A bright, new author. Story full of courage, adventure, and enchantment.

—Leah Williams, educator,
Oregon City, Oregon

This book will take young readers on a fantastical journey to a world full of imagination, courage, and triumph. In addition, Harrington's own story as a writer may even inspire her young readers to pick up that pen (or laptop) to discover the wonder of writing for themselves.

—Dara Kramer, sixth–grade teacher,
Oregon City School District

Griffin's Calling contained both realistic and fantasy fiction. My favorite part was when Griffin first met the Critins. I liked the book because of its great descriptions, but it wasn't difficult to read.

—Jeremy Carnahan, fifth–grade student,
Beavercreek Elementary

GRIFFIN'S
CALLING

GRIFFIN'S
CALLING

by N.R. Harrington

TATE PUBLISHING & *Enterprises*

Published by Tate Publishing & Enterprises, LLC
127 E. Trade Center Terrace | Mustang, Oklahoma 73064 USA
1.888.361.9473 | www.tatepublishing.com

Tate Publishing is committed to excellence in the publishing industry. The company reflects the philosophy established by the founders, based on Psalm 68:11,
"The Lord gave the word and great was the company of those who published it."

Book design copyright © 2010 by Tate Publishing, LLC. All rights reserved.
Cover & design by Lindsay B. Behrens
Illustration by Lauren Judah

Published in the United States of America

ISBN: 978-1-61566-694-2
Juvenile Fiction / Fantasy & Magic
10.01.12

ACKNOWLEDGMENTS

I would like to show much gratitude toward my mother for the creation of this novel. Without her constant support, faith in me, and optimistic outlook, this would not have been possible. Also, I would like to give recognition to my father for his never–ending support and encouragement throughout my life. A special thanks goes out to Carol Hirons for being one of the first to read and help edit *Griffin's Calling* and for advising me to stay with it. Also, a big thank you to Redland Elementary's fifth– and sixth–grade reading class. They were the first group of children to read this novel, and they greatly encouraged me to write a sequel. And a huge thanks to all my crazy friends who probably thought I was the crazy one for writing a book but always supported me in writing it. And last, a tribute goes out to singer and songwriter Billy Joel for inspiring me with his song "River of Dreams" and the band Toto for their hit "Africa."

—N.R. Harrington

FOREWORD

"Mom, I'm going to write a novel," N.R. exclaimed as she came home from school and lacrosse practice that spring day of her sophomore year in high school.

"Okay…" I said, not wanting to discourage her but disbelieving what she stated to me that day in May of 2007.

N.R. had always been a good writer and had won writing awards during her sophomore year at high school, but writing a novel I thought was way over her head.

Next thing I knew the following week she showed me fifteen pages of her "novel" written on the back of homework pages. I read it and was impressed with what I saw but not too happy it was done during her social studies class.

Well if she was determined to write, she needed at least a notebook to write it down in, so we bought her a spiral note book, and she rewrote the beginnings of her book. Again being fascinated with her aspirations and the contents of the book, I showed it to a colleague at work who is a fabulous writer and writing teacher. Carol Hirons was impressed with what she read and told N.R. she was dying to know what happens next and to keep up the great work.

N.R. wrote that entire following summer, writing late in to the night, taking her notebook on vacations. (Her waterfall scene was inspired by the powerful, majestic falls at Yellowstone National Park, and the name Sable came from a fish she saw at an aquarium called Sable Fish.)

Writing the novel was fun for N.R. and especially for me. I have been a Reading Specialist for the Oregon City School District for twenty–two years. I have been teaching struggling readers in grades K–9 for most of my life and really love it! Of course I love to read so I was able to edit and guide her story. Mother/daughter relationships can be tumultuous especially in the teenage years, and ours was no exception. I found that this novel was something we could communicate about and enjoy together even when times were rough.

She wrote during her whole junior year in high school. She was determined not to quit when she got really busy with her sports, homework, and of course her social life. N.R. later stated that her biggest fear was *not* finishing it. And of course she was asking me, "Mom, do you really think it is good enough to be published?"

Before long she had hand written 120 pages in her notebook. We bought her a laptop before her senior year. She rewrote and edited her story on her laptop. She was pretty funny, saying, "Wow, it really needed editing." I of course told her her writing had matured and so had she in the course of the book.

We gave the first five chapters to friends and colleagues. I knew by now that N.R.'s story was quite special, but I was floored by the reactions of all the readers. They absolutely loved it and wanted to know the rest of the story.

N.R. finished it in the winter of 2008/09, while I busily searched the world of publishing. Looking at many Web sites and learning all I could about getting a novel published, I felt a bit discouraged seeing how rare it was to get a new author published and the process as a whole. Late February, we found Tate Publishing. We read that they will read a new author's manuscript. So N.R. sent it in hoping they would enjoy reading it as much as she enjoyed creating it.

Meanwhile I had the *real* test audience ahead of me. I decided to print N.R.'s manuscript and read it with my fifth– and sixth–grade reading students. These are reluctant reading students having individual reading problems, such as word attack skills, comprehensions issues, ADHD, and so on. These kids were the ones that she wrote the book for and hoped to inspire to enjoy reading. Well, they were absolutely nuts about the story. They never wanted the reading period to end; they begged to take the book home to finish it on their own. It was fantastic for me to see their reaction to the manuscript. And I had a ball making up activities and comprehension questions to go with the story. We even wrote persuasive letters to the publisher stating reasons why they should publish it (though we didn't send them). Also they begged for a sequel, and they were thrilled when N.R. came in and discussed the book with them. One of my former reading students needed to find a fantasy genre book for his sixth–grade class. I gave him a copy of the manuscript, and he looked at it quite reluctantly because it of course did not look like a "genuine" book. I made a bet with him. I said if he read the first five chapters and he was bored and brought it back to me not finished I owed him a soda. But if he couldn't put it down, he just had to finish it, he owed me a soda. Well a week later he came into my classroom bringing me a diet coke. He said, "You were right. I'm on chapter nine, and I love it and have to finish it."

On May 5, 2009, N.R. had the day of her life. She had a twenty–two–page document in the mail from Tate Publishing, offering her a contract for royalties for her book *Griffin's Calling*. This was a very exciting day indeed. But she also had a big Lacrosse game ahead of her that evening against our biggest rival. She had the game of her life scoring ten goals! (Her team later on that month became state champions.)

Her father and I are very proud of N.R.'s accomplishments. She looks forward to going to college, playing lacrosse, and writing the sequel to *Griffin's Calling*.

We all hope you enjoy this novel as much as she did writing and creating it. Thanks to all the encouragement along the way from friends, colleagues, and family members. I think we all have our own callings in life, and like Griffin, we are all just trying to find our way.

Sincerely,
Michelle Harrington
Reading Specialist
Oregon City School District
Oregon City, Oregon

GRIFFIN'S
CALLING

RED LIGHT

In the town of Oakridge, Oregon, where the rain sank deep into the earth's roots, causing trees to grow tall and stout, a young boy longed for adventure. As he slid his window open to sneak out of his home, he did not know where he was going or where he wanted to go. He spent most of his nights this way—searching, wondering, and wanting something more, something extraordinary. The boy needed to know what he was in search of. He was just hoping something would pop out at him, like a jack–in–the–box, but possibly not even that, for he didn't want the music to guide him to when the clown would burst out. He had a craving for unpredictability. The wandering boy did this the majority of his troubled nights, yet he seemed to return home feeling the same way he left. Prying the window open, he made a crack just big enough to fit through. He cleared the window with ease because he had done this many times. The boy hit the ground, making little sound, and started his way toward the backyard woods. At sixteen, Griffin Dominic was nearly an adult, but he had the imagination of a child. Very often he let his mind take him into unbelievable worlds. Griffin dreamed about life outside the skies and worlds beneath the oceans. He had straight, shaggy hair as black as a raven's feathers and brown, worried eyes. The moonlight shined down upon the path he was following. Stuffing his hands in his pockets, Griffin looked curiously about the premises. In his surroundings, the boy felt comfortable and at ease. He cleared the path a bit, kicking twigs and stones off to the side.

A sharp beep sounded in the silent night. Looking at his wrist, Griffin saw it was midnight. Having thought it was merely ten o'clock, Griffin realized he had lost track of time. Disappointed, he started wandering back home. As he walked home, he began to think in astonishment of how completely different he was than his parents. He had been going on these night adventures for almost the past year now, and his parents still had no knowledge of him doing so. Griffin's parents did not understand him, nor did they make an effort to. His father, David Dominic, was the sort of fellow who believed in hard work and dedication. He was a rugged man with broad shoulders. His black eyes would even put fright into the devil's soul. The boy's mother, on the other hand, was eccentric and insensible. You could convince her that your food was talking to you at the dinner table, and she would ask, "What did it say?"

Her short, curly hair and purple glasses made her quite a sight to see. Griffin was nothing like his mother and even more so unlike his father. This boy was a quick–witted lad who enjoyed nothing more than getting away with the impossible. He could snatch a sleeping lion's bone out from under its nose, and it wouldn't even faze the beast.

Griffin's rebellious nature made it difficult for him to have and keep friends. And even when he finally did make a friend or two, he always seemed to find mischief with them. Never making friends with the right sort caused Griffin to spend many hours in the principal's office. At school one afternoon, the teacher had to practically tear apart Griffin and another boy, for they were going at each other like crazed dogs. It started when a boy made fun of Griffin's ear piercings. "You look like a little girl with those things in," he shouted at Griffin.

After the fight had been broken up, Griffin decided he needed to send one more punch the boy's way. Pretending to walk away from his foe, Griffin quickly jolted toward him. With the force of a hammer, he pounded his fist into the face of the unaware boy, hitting him square in the nose. The surprised boy crashed to the ground, contorting his face in agony. Griffin turned around and smiled. Once again, he was sent to the principal's office. To stop Griffin's bleeding, Principal Mrs. Manor handed him a tissue. This lady was small and dreadfully polite. She had white, frizzy hair and cherry lipstick that glistened when the light shone.

Griffin had never thought her to be the principal type, for she was exceptionally forgiving. She set her coffee to the side of her desk and sighed. "Griffin, you need to take up some kind of hobby, something that releases your anger and takes your mind off getting into fights with the other boys."

Later, Mrs. Manor spoke a few words to his parents about his mishaps and gave them a list of activities that Griffin could take part in. The boy's parents, of course, thought it a brilliant idea for Griffin to get a hobby. Griffin was not too keen to this *brilliant* idea. After his parents—mostly his father—scolded him, the argument ended with a month's grounding and Griffin being forced to take archery classes. He would be attending classes from a neighbor down the road who had practically been born with a bow in his hand. At first Griffin refused to attend his lessons, and he regularly would retreat to his woods when it was time for class. "You *will* go to those lessons, or you're going to surely regret it," his father would threaten, fist shaking and face reddened. "You're worthless, Griffin!"

Finally, after much confrontation with his father, he realized that not going to a few lessons wasn't worth being grounded for the rest of his life. Griffin would never admit this to his parents, but after going to a few lessons, he actually loved the thought of shooting a pointed arrow through an object. He adored the way it felt when he released the spear–like arrow through the air.

A few months later, Griffin was making and selling bows and arrows to the kids at school. He was making quite a profit doing this, but his bow–selling days ended when boys began to shoot them on school grounds.

Lost in thought, Griffin ventured into a part of the woods he had never set foot on. He was brought back to reality by a red, laser–like glare in a distant part of the forest. *Is my mind playing tricks on me?* he thought. The red light started to fade away into the hazy, moonlit night. Griffin, longing to know what this glowing radiance was, started to tear through the woods after it. Not having a flashlight to show his path, Griffin stumbled over the sturdy tree roots and twigs. He struggled to stay on his feet. Sprinting, chasing, crashing through the forest floor, the light became fainter. Determined not to give up, he ran more rapidly, but regrettably with every step he took, the light became less visible until it was completely out of sight. Lost and enraged, Griffin trailed through the trees to get home. Griffin pondered, *What was that light? Where did it come from? And why was it in these abandoned woods?* All questions he had no answers to.

After an hour of sticker bushes grabbing at his legs, he was at last home. Griffin climbed through his window. Like pieces falling from a punctured balloon, he collapsed on his bed. The exhausted boy fell asleep knowing he would be back to the woods the next night.

A NEW COMPANION

Griffin was awakened the next morning by his father shaking him. He was already running late for his weekly archery lesson. "Get a move on! It's already eleven o'clock!" his father demanded, exiting his room. His mother's egg and ham breakfast was teasing his nose, which caused him to quickly spring upward. But it was too fast. He had forgotten what had happened the night before. Running through the unforgiving woods at full tread in nothing but knee–high shorts had done a great deal to his legs. He soaked a towel in water and gently placed it on his throbbing, scratched legs. Griffin's father burst into his room once more hollering, "You need to hurry up! And what in the world happened to your legs?"

"Well, I was just getting my arrows that I had been shooting in the woods, and the blackberry bushes got in my way," Griffin lied.

"Well, it looks like someone took a dang weed whacker to you, boy. We best get a move on if you want to be on time. Now hurry up! I have better things to do." David slammed the door behind him.

Griffin lightly dabbed his reddened legs one last time, winced, then threw the rag into the sink. As he undressed, his clothes revealed brown dirt smudges from the eventful night before. He changed into a black T–shirt and a pair of dark blue Levi's.

Griffin sat down at the breakfast table with his parents. "Here you go, Griffy," his mom said, handing him a plate of steaming breakfast.

His mother, Mary Dominic, was wearing her usual pink pajama pants, white robe, and purple slippers. Her hair was bound up in curlers, and it looked as if a bird would claim it as its nest at any moment. The boy took the plate from her hand and sat down. Fork in hand, he began to twirl it around in the egg yolk, making a yellow mess. Forgetting the presence of his parents, the boy sat there thinking, wanting, and needing to know what that shining jewel was in the darkness. Griffin wondered, *Was it aliens or something?* Feeling foolish, Griffin realized that maybe his need to find something more in life actually caused his imaginative mind to see such a wonder. Generating deeper thought now, he asked himself, *I live in a small town in the middle of nowhere. No one comes out that far, no one. There aren't many houses out here, especially the parts of the woods that I was searching. Were my eyes really playing tricks on me?*

David noticed his son dozing off. He kicked his left shin, causing Griffin to yelp in pain. David, smirking at Griffin's discomfort, exclaimed, "Wake up, boy! And suck it up!"

Looking disgusted, Griffin hurriedly left his seat and grabbed his uneaten and once desirable meal. He walked over to the blue tiled countertop and slammed his plate on it, causing egg yolk to splatter about the counter. He then made his way to the front door and declared, "I'll be waiting in the car!" With a quick tug, he forcefully closed the door behind him.

Confused, Mary asked, "What's going on, David?"

David clenched his fist and smashed his hand on the table. As he left to meet Griffin in the car, David muttered, "Something's not right in that boy's mind." David sat down in the driver's seat. Griffin didn't have his license or his permit; his parents wouldn't allow it until they saw "more responsibility" in him. Realizing his son was in the back seat instead of riding shotgun, David snapped, "What's wrong with you?"

Griffin muttered, "You." Not a word left their lips for the rest of the car ride. Griffin was happy for the silence; all he wanted to imagine was the mysterious red light.

The car screeched to a stop at John Carton's home. This house was small and looked like a cottage from a fairy tale. The home had a peaceful sense about it, and when taking the time to realize the tranquility it held, one might never want to leave. John Carton was the sort of man who was up to any challenge. He was open minded and not quick to judge. Griffin appreciated these traits and respected John for having them. John could work wonders with a bow. One would think he had been raised with a bow in his hand for all his days. John was a giant, but a gentle one at that.

Griffin jumped out of the car with his bow, relieved to get out of the presence of his father. Before a word was said, Griffin shut the car door. David ripped out of the driveway, leaving a cloud of dust. Knocking on the front door, Griffin stepped back and admired the welcoming nature of the house. In the flowerbeds along the house walls were red roses. You would think the sweet scent of flowers had jumped right off the petals and onto your nose. Griffin had a soft spot for nature. He was infatuated with the way he felt when it was just him and the trees. Lying under the comforting arms of the forest and listening to nothing but birds singing was a lullaby to him. He adored the days when the soft winds blew through the treetops and lightly aired his face; that was his paradise.

With a bow in each hand, John opened the door. Smiling, he yelled, "You ready, Griff!"

"When am I not!"

Looking down at the two bows John was holding, Griffin asked, "Is someone else joining us today, John? Cuz I brought my bow." Griffin recognized the bow in John's left hand; it was the usual plain, brown, and wooden bow with scruffy edges and a worn–out look to it. The bow in his right hand he did not recognize. The other bow was beautiful. Holding the bows in both of his oversized hands, Griffin could tell the difference between the two crafts. The dazzling bow was wooden with gold trim around it. About the edges, where the gold trim did not touch, the words *Steady Eye and Fire* were engraved. Its dimensions in length and width were smaller than Griffin's bow.

Ignoring Griffin's question, John said, "This is a shortbow."

"What's a shor—"

Before Griffin could mutter another word, John interrupted, "A shortbow is an unusual kind of bow. It's shorter than your average bow and shoots much smaller arrows."

Griffin had his head tilted to one side. "But what's so great about smaller arrows?"

"These little devils..." John walked back into the house and began to rustle through some boxes he kept in a small room. Griffin waited in wonderment. He returned to the front door holding a quiver stuffed with arrows. The quiver was brown and had a leather strap to fling across your shoulders. The many arrows were not the usual arrows that they had been working with. They were much stockier and had rock tips that looked to be unbreakable. "...will release harder, faster, and stronger than the regular arrows that we have been using. These suckers are capable of incredible penetration. Let's just say one blow to your stomach with one of these, and it wouldn't be a pretty sight. Come on; I'll show you what this thing can do!" Closing the door, they made their way to the back of the house, where there were acres of trees as far as the eye could see.

As soon as they set foot into the woods, the temperature dropped drastically, and all sunlight faded into gray. Griffin and John followed a dirt trail in the dense forest. They were thankful for the cool air, for the blistering summer rays were getting to them. The thick forest branches served as the ideal shelter from the sun, only allowing speckles of sunlight to peer in. Nearing the end of the path was a large, rounded clearing. Surrounding the clearing on all sides were red and white targets dangling from the arms of trees, high, low, near, and far. There were already a few arrows pierced in them from their previous lessons. This was a bowman's paradise. John hurled the quiver full of arrows off his back. He took a shortbow arrow and set the tail of it on the bow's tight string. He then carefully aimed the sharp tip at a nearby target, pulled back and let it go. The arrow was but a quick blur cutting through the air. He hit the target directly in the red center. At impact, the target exploded like a missile penetrating a meager cottage. White and red wooden shards dropped to the ground. Mouth agape, Griffin smiled in shock. "Me next!"

Proudly John declared, "Not bad, huh? Yes, you're next, Griffin."

Griffin took the shortbow and gazed at it in admiration. "Now, Griffin," John started. Don't be getting all discouraged if you don't fancy the bow too much at first. It took me a great deal of hard work before I could even dream about hitting the outer edges of these here targets with that there bow."

John had barely finished his sympathy speech before Griffin pulled back on the bow's tough strings and set the arrow free. Whistling through the air, the arrow was dialed on the most difficult target of the training ground. The dartlike missile drilled directly through the stagnant target. Once again, shards of red and white floated peacefully to the soil. "Not bad, huh?" Griffin smirked.

Eyes widened in disbelief, John exclaimed, "Man! I am a *good* teacher!"

"Hah, maybe I'm just a natural," Griffin boasted.

Trying not to be too surprised with how well he had done, Griffin grabbed another arrow from the quiver. To make sure what he accomplished wasn't just beginner's luck, he reset the arrow. Aiming for a shorter distance target, he pulled back and released. The powerful arrow hit its destination, destroying another one. "Woo! That's what I'm talking about!" Griffin proudly said, throwing up his arms.

With a smile the size of a crescent moon, John announced, "It looks like this bow has found its new owner."

"What? What are you talking about?"

"The bow is yours."

"Mine? You're giving this bow to me? I mean...wow, thank you, thanks a lot! But are you sure you want to give *this* to me?" Griffin said in awe.

"Without a doubt in my mind, this bow belongs in your hands, Griff. My father would often tell me as a young lad that I got a certain 'look' in my eyes whenever I had that in my hands," John explained while pointing at the unique shortbow. I wasn't sure what he spoke of back then, but now I see you, and I know exactly what he was talking about. You have that same look in your eyes, Griffin."

Gripping the precious bow tighter, Griffin declared, "I will guard this with my life." Reaching down, Griffin grabbed another arrow. He positioned it on the bow. Once more he took aim and let loose, bursting yet another round target.

"You owe me three targets now," John joked.

After two hours of bow practice, they started treading back though the dimming forest.

Back at the house, the two of them chatted over a Coke and cookies. When listening to their conversation, one would think they were lifelong friends. They talked about problems, happiness, and life in general. This was just what Griffin needed to take his mind off his father. "You don't fancy your dad much now, do you?" John started.

Nearly spitting out his drink, Griffin laughed. "Let's just say I walk in wide, *very* wide circles around him."

"Oh, I see. Well not too long from now and you'll be out of the nest, boy." He chuckled, softly punching Griffin in the shoulder.

"Not soon enough." Griffin sighed.

What seemed like ten minutes had actually been an hour of conversation between the two. Griffin heard his dad tearing up the driveway. David never showed up late to anything, and now, knowing Griffin actually enjoyed his lessons, he made more of an effort to retrieve Griffin precisely on time. Griffin looked up to the sky and asked, "Why me?"

He gathered his two bows and began to get out of the chair. "Don't forget these!" reminded John, handing him the quiver of shortbow arrows.

"Oh yeah! And thanks again. I won't let this bow out of my sight!" he reassured John with a smile.

Griffin started his unfortunate walk to the car, where his father waited. David impatiently laid on the horn. Struck with remembrance, Griffin quickly spun around toward John and said, "Hey, John, I meant to ask you this earlier."

"Yes?" John wondered.

"Why is *Steady Eye and Fire* engraved into this bow?" Griffin questioned while showing the bow to John.

John smiled. "Ahhh, thought you might be asking that. Well, when I was a young bowman such as you, my father often told me, 'Son, just keep a steady eye and fire.' I don't have the best memory, and his helpful saying would always seem to slip my mind. So, to help me remember, my father engraved it on the bow. By doing this he hoped that every time I pulled back on those strings"—he nodded at the shortbow—"I would see these words and remember to keep a steady eye. I always shot better after my father did this. So, Griffin, before letting the arrow go, glance up at those words, and the arrow will take itself where you want it to go."

Smiling, Griffin replied, "Will do, sir."

"You better get a move on before your pa throws a fit."

These words had barely left his lips before David came storming up to Griffin and John. "Where the heck have you been, Griffin? I've been waiting in the car for almost five minutes! You know your class ends at five and not a moment later!" David roared, his face flushed.

"It's my fault really." John intervened while getting out of the chair. "I lost track of time. We ran late today."

"You just stay out of this. This is between me and my boy. Griffin should know what time he gets done. He doesn't need someone telling him! I wish you would grow up and grow up fast."

Anger billowing up inside, John exclaimed, "You listen here. Griffin is a great boy, and he doesn't need anyone, especially you, telling him otherwise. I told you it was my fault the boy was late!"

"Yeah, well…You…"

"Stop! Let's just go! C'mon; let's just go," Griffin interrupted.

Sneering at John, David tugged on Griffin's shirt. "Now get in the car!" Griffin followed David to the front of the house. "You best not pull something like that again," David said while the two got in the car.

David's frustrated eyes were focused on the road.

"All right, all right." Griffin didn't want to agree, but he worried if he didn't his stubborn father wouldn't let him see John anymore for lessons.

David flashed his eyes toward Griffin's leg, which was hiding the shortbow in between the door. "What's that?" David questioned while he glanced at the road and back to the short-bow. Trying to hide his new precious belonging, Griffin pushed it down to the car floor by his feet next to the quiver of arrows.

"What's what?" he replied, trying to act surprised.

"What are you hiding, boy?" David gripped the wheel with one hand and, reaching across Griffin's lap, snatched the shortbow.

"Give it back!" Griffin shouted in dismay.

"What do we have here?" he exclaimed with an evil smirk. "A new toy from that wacko John?"

Wishing now that he had sat in the backseat, Griffin replied, "That wacko is more of a person and a father than you'll ever be."

"Oh really, Griff?"

"Yeah really, and don't call me Griff."

"I'll call you whatever I see fit. Also, Griff," David added while rolling down his window, "you're *never* going back to those lessons again."

David acquired a tighter grip on the vibrant bow. Raising his arm that held the weapon, he thrust the bow out of the moving vehicle like a boomerang.

"What are you doing?" Griffin's eyes were wide with shock. "You're insane! Let me out of this car *now!*"

"You want out? I'll let you *out!*"

David punched his foot on the brakes. Griffin was sent flying toward the dashboard until his seatbelt caught him and slammed him back into the seat. The car came to an abrupt stop, causing smoke to arise from the tires. Griffin took his old bow and quiver of arrows and hurriedly reached for the car door handle. Closing the car door, Griffin remarked to his father, "Don't be expecting me home tonight."

Before David got a word to Griffin, the angered boy shut the door behind him. He left David not knowing that this would be the last time he would talk to his father in over a year.

NOT HUMAN

Griffin ran along the dusty road like a dog searching for his lost ball. He was panic stricken. He had made a promise to take care of this precious possession. What if he got to the bow and it was all tattered and ruined? Griffin thought to himself, *John just stood up to my father to help me out. This is how I'm going to repay him? By losing his most prized possession that he just gave me?* In every step he took, waves of fear hit him harder and harder. The power of his trampling feet caused the strap of the quiver to slip off his back. It tumbled to the ground, causing the shortbow arrows to scatter about the gravel road. Griffin came to a sudden stop, almost tripping from the loose rocks beneath. "Oh just perfect!"

A few minutes later Griffin nearly had all of the arrows back in the quiver. As he was picking up the last fallen arrow, something caught his eye. Using his left hand as a visor, the boy saw a shimmering object farther down the road. Coming closer now, he realized it was his short-bow that his father had carelessly discarded. Leaping for joy, Griffin ran faster toward it, taking in quick strides. He took the valued bow in hand and scanned every inch of it in hopes it was in the same condition in which it was given to him. Realizing that it was unscathed, he released a sigh of relief. "Thank God."

He began to retrace his steps, wondering where his next move would be. *Maybe I could go back to John's house. He would take me in no doubt!* He pondered to himself. But he decided against it, for he didn't want to cause any more trouble in John's life than he already had today. Going to a friend's house was also out of the question.

Twilight was rapidly approaching, and Griffin stood facing the very forest that led to his house. Like a wave crashing on the ocean's rocks, he was struck with an idea. *My forest, that's where I'll go; I can handle a night in the forest.* If he was truly going to bear a night in the woods, Griffin decided he would be needing a flashlight. He wasn't going to make the same mistake twice. How could he acquire such a thing though? With the mishap that had happened today with John, he could not show a single hair on his head to his father. Griffin would have to sneak in his home unseen and grab his flashlight. Being the sneaky fellow that he was, Griffin was quite confident that he could achieve this goal.

After a forty–five–minute trek, Griffin was back at home. Darkness had well overcome the night. He swiftly hid his bows and quiver in a nearby bush and made his way to the back door. Slowly opening the door, Griffin slipped inside, making no sound. He faced the hallway his room was on about two doors down. Tiptoeing ever so carefully down the hallway to his room, the boy could see his father at the couch with a beer in his hand. David sat yelling some murderous nonsense at the ballgame he was glued to. He could hear his mother working away in the kitchen. She was preparing her infamous fish soup, and the smell was nearly too much for Griffin to bear.

He made it to his room unheard. The boy ventured to his dresser and pulled out the first drawer. The thought of David catching him entered his mind, and out of nervousness he pulled the drawer clean out of the dresser. It crashed to the ground surely allowing everyone in the household to hear it. "No!" Griffin hastily whispered under his breath. Snatching his flashlight, he retreated to his closet and listened for his alarmed parents to enter the room. He could hear David approaching. Griffin's heart thumped harder and harder with every step his father gained toward his room. The boy gazed through the opening in the closet. He saw his father enter. David stared at the fallen drawer. Looking about the area for a sign of movement David spotted a twenty–dollar bill. David pocketed the money and grinned. David didn't seem to care about the mysterious fallen drawer anymore. He exited the room.

Letting out a sigh of relief, Griffin cautiously freed himself of the closet. He snatched a black sweater from the disorderly floor and tiptoed to the window. With his flashlight in hand, he slid the window upward and quietly slipped through the modest opening. After some time, he reclaimed his hidden belongings and began to venture toward the forest he so often visited.

Trailing through the woods, the boy gazed past the treetops at the cloudless night. Still very concerned, Griffin wondered what he was going to do if he couldn't go to John's for more lessons. John was the only one who truly understood Griffin. He looked about the dark environment. Griffin jerked his head back at the sight of what appeared to be the same red light in which he had seen the previous night. Determined now more than ever, Griffin flicked on the flashlight and once again attempted to chase down the mystifying light. Running at full sprint, the boy could tell he was drawing nearer. Actually being able to see this time, Griffin was much swifter and could move through the forest with ease. The light became more vibrant as he became closer, and he slowed his tired legs down to a silent walk. The light was not going away this time, and Griffin became hopeful that he might actually solve this mystery. Hiding quietly behind a tree, he peaked his curious face around it. The boy saw two figures walking around. The red light was hanging about one of their necks. He could hear the two squabbling.

"Will you listen to me for once? Sable, the diamond isn't safe! It's not going to be safe anywhere until they are stopped. We must act quickly before all hope is lost!"

"The diamond is safe here! Why else would I bring it to this unfamiliar land? *They* don't have the slightest knowledge of this place!"

While eavesdropping, many thoughts floated through Griffin's mind. *The diamond must be what is hanging around his neck. What others are they speaking of? Who are the others?*

"And how do we be certain the Shriekian are unaware of this secret? They could have found this place just as we have! And when they do, if they already have not claimed this land, we will have nowhere to retreat, no place to hide. We must battle for our right to exist! We must fight until we can fight no more."

"Fight?" questioned the shadow bearing the red light. "Fight with what? Whom? Our assembly of fifty warriors? I refuse to take my soldiers into a war that *cannot* be won!"

"War?" Griffin whispered in puzzlement.

"So…we run. We hide like cowards? If we continue to live like this, it will just be a matter of time before our kind will all be slaughtered! Slaughtered until what? Until you and I are the only ones who stand in this forsaken place? We need to search for their weakness, fight them…do something!"

Just as soon as the other had finished, the being with the glowing light shouted, "They have *no* weakness! If so, we would not be sitting here! Our race has lost lives in search of the Shriekian weakness! I tried to stop them.

He just wouldn't listen to me … Vector was lost to those beasts! They are bred to dominate, nothing more. No more blood will be shed over something that cannot be found!"

"Sable, let the past be the past. The amount of blood that will be shed is destined to be less if we take action."

"Well, this is my plan of action."

Being so engaged in listening to the conversation, Griffin didn't realize that half of his body was hanging out from the protecting tree. The shadow not bearing the necklace of light caught a glimpse of Griffin's shadow. The unknown being began to gaze more intently in Griffin's direction. Griffin, realizing he was seen, jumped behind the tree and out of their sight.

"What? What did you see?" questioned the one called Sable.

With a distraught feeling inside of him, the unsure shadow said in a low voice, "I saw something. S–something behind that tree! Let's leave now."

"What happened to not running?" Pulling out a knife from a leather waistband, the carrier of the red light edged closer to the tree that Griffin was hidden behind. Griffin saw the light of the necklace glowing closer and closer to him. He grabbed an arrow from his quiver and got his shortbow ready for action.

"Show yourself!" the approaching being demanded. "Show yourself! You have been seen! Step out from there!"

Weapon in hand, Griffin was ready to do damage. Sable was but two feet away from the tree sheltering the boy. Thoughts of making a run for it went through Griffin's mind, but if he ran now, he would regret it for the rest of his days. Deciding to be bold, he stepped out from the tree and aimed his arrow directly at the approaching being.

Griffin immediately realized the unknown person carried a weapon of his own, and he demanded, "Put the knife down."

Dropping the weapon to the ground, the shadow smoothly replied, "You're only a human."

Trying to keep his cool, Griffin said uneasily, "Yeah...you're not?"

To give Griffin a better look at his face, he raised the glowing necklace with what appeared to be a feathered arm and replied, "Not exactly."

SAYING GOOD-BYE

The face of the unknown was anything but human. Terrified, Griffin looked into the cat-like eyes of the creature. It had a short beak of an eagle and a long, forked tongue. It owned a pair of horns that jutted backward from the top of its head. The creature's claws appeared sharp and unforgiving. Sticking out from the back of the being was a pair of wings. It also had a lengthy lion tail. Frightened at what he had just seen, Griffin stumbled backward, his arrow still pointed at the birdlike thing. "What are you?" Griffin hollered.

Without saying a word, the animal drew closer to Griffin, now only inches away from the sharp arrow. "I swear to you…you…you alien! Take one more step, and I'll drive this arrow straight through your head!"

While stepping even closer to Griffin, the being smirked, "Watch your back, boy."

Griffin quickly spun around. As soon as he faced the other direction, a cloud of purple dust was blown straight into Griffin's unsuspecting face. Coughing, the boy attempted to make a dash for home. Then, like a lightning strike, it hit him. Griffin was suddenly overtaken by a sensation of tiredness. Darkness overcame him, and he collapsed to the ground as limp and motionless as a corpse.

Griffin awakened to find his wrists separately bound by vines to the same tree that he had taken refuge behind. Terrified, he yelled for help, but there was no use, for he was in an uninhabited part of the forest. "I should have run the second I saw those two," he muttered with regret.

Stricken with fear, thoughts of being abducted and tested on by aliens raced through his mind. Griffin tried to slide his wrists out from the vine's clutches. Despite his effort, with every tug, the vine got much tighter until Griffin's blood flow was nearly cut off.

"You don't want to be doing that," warned an unseen voice.

Just then the two creatures came pushing through some nearby bushes. "He speaks the truth," announced the one carrying the diamond. "Last fellow who tested those vines had his hand squeezed clean off."

Since it was now daylight, Griffin could see much more of the beings. They were a bit taller than Griffin and had a ten–foot wingspan. Their bodies were completely consumed in golden feathers with the exception of a patch of black feathers on their chest. Sharp talons for their feet served as a perfect defensive mechanism. Quickly getting to his feet, the boy stuttered, "Look…I don't know what you are, but if you let me go, I'll stay out of your woods forever. Please let me go!"

"What is your name, boy?" the one possessing the red jewel asked.

Thinking they might let him go if he did as they said, he stated, "Griffin…Griffin Dominic."

"Well hello, Mr. Griffin. I'm Sable, and this is Mogol," the diamond carrier exclaimed.

Letting curiosity get the better of him, Griffin questioned, "What are you? And what's with that diamond around your neck?"

Shaking his head from left to right, Mogol said, "He's already heard too much, Sable. We cannot get mixed up with another human."

"How long were you listening to us last night? Sable demanded.

Realizing he had said too much, Griffin lied. "Oh, only about a minute or so. I couldn't even understand what you two were talking about anyways."

Sable knew what must be done. "You know what to do, Mogol." Sable sighed.

"Yes." Mogol slid a double–sided knife out of his waistband.

"What? No! No, listen, I didn't hear anything! I don't know *anything!* Don't do this!" pleaded Griffin.

Sable disappeared into the forest, for he didn't want to witness such a scene. "I'm sorry, boy," Mogol said with a saddened voice.

Once more trying to break free of the vines, the boy pulled harder on them, which caused them to close down on his wrists even harder. As Griffin fell down in agony, Mogol grabbed him by his hair and held the foreboding knife inches from his throat. Griffin begged, "Please don't kill me! Please! I can help your kind! There was a war you spoke of last night!"

"What would a human have to offer? Humans are foolish and weak." Mogol released Griffin's hair and drew back the knife.

Relieved to have the knife out of his face, Griffin hurriedly thought of how he could possibly help these beings. "Well...I..."

Looking around hastily for a clue, his eyes landed upon his abandoned shortbow about ten feet away from him. *That's it,* he thought.

"Speak up! How could you possibly be any use to us?" the feathered creature questioned.

"Well, I could make weapons for you! You see those objects just over there?" the boy said while pointing to his two bows and quiver.

"Yes, just some human nonsense."

"Have you ever even seen something like that before last night?" Griffin questioned, gaining some confidence.

"No. What are you getting at, Griffin? Griffin's the name, right?"

Nodding his head yes, he asked, "Can I show you something? Just give me my belongings back, and I'll show you how you will win your war."

Mogol then gathered up Griffin's weapons and set them at his feet. "Impress me, human," Mogol said, holding his knife toward Griffin once more. "And no games!"

Taking his shortbow in his reddened hand, Griffin set up an arrow. He then spotted a rotting tree stump but a few yards away. His wrists were in much pain, and he was greatly nervous with the presence of the razor sharp knife, but Griffin was too great of a bowman to let these things distract him. He took aim at the lifeless wood and set the arrow free. It penetrated the decomposing stump at full force. The stump was cleanly split down the middle in two halves. Mogol stood awed at the sight he had just witnessed. "Impressed?" Griffin asked, self–assured.

With his knife still threatening to pierce Griffin's skin, Mogol stated, "Well...we may just have *some* use for you."

To make sure Griffin was defenseless, Mogol took back the boy's weapons before drawing his knife away.

"I swear, if you don't kill me, I will do whatever I can for your kind. I can help you win your war," Griffin pleaded.

"You show our kind how to use that skill, and we shall spare you. You lead us to a victory, and you Griffin...you will be treated as a God."

"Why haven't you got rid of this human yet?"

Spinning around to face Sable, Mogol shouted, "Sable! I found our way to beat the Shriekian! If you will do so much as to see what this young man has to offer, you will be very pleased!"

"I do recall hearing that we were not getting mixed up with another human, do you not?" Sable smugly replied.

"Yes, but Sable, sir. Just let him show…"

"No! Don't be so foolish to think that we can bring him home just as we brought her. I can also remember what happened last time we brought a human to our land, can you not? Or has your memory faded?"

Griffin was getting rather anxious, and many questions were building up inside of him. "There was someone else? I…I mean another human?" Griffin asked.

Ignoring the curious boy, Mogol started, "Please, Sable, give it a chance. One chance, and if you don't like what you see…the boy dies."

Sable pondered to himself for a few moments and sighed. "One chance and nothing more."

Mogol then supplied Griffin with his bow and a single arrow. "Well, you know, this task would be much easier if my wrists weren't bound so tightly with these vines," complained Griffin.

"The vines will do!" Sable snapped back.

"Right," the boy said and began looking for a target.

Pulling out a knife from his belt, Sable threatened, "Hurry up, boy."

Scanning the premises, Griffin spotted a tree branch about twenty feet away from them. With a quick release, the arrow soared freely through the air until hitting the stagnant branch and splitting it in two pieces. Sable stared at the divided wood. Griffin hoped and prayed what he had just performed had pleased the diamond bearer. After a few seconds of silent disbelief, Sable announced with a smile, "We may just have something here."

Mogol raised his hands in joy and exclaimed, "He's absolutely perfect, as if a gift sent from the great one himself!"

"Yes, this is truly a gift. He will be an excellent guardian of the diamond," Sable added, nodding his feathered head.

Mogol's smile drained from his face. "Are you blind? Can you not see the opportunity we have been presented with? Let us use this secret for war!"

"I will not take us to war! He shall come with us, but only for the protection of the diamond and ourselves! Now, son, we shall spare your life if you swear to protect this here gem with the best of your ability. What say you? Will you come?"

"Doesn't look like I have much of a choice, now does it?" Griffin remarked.

"All right then, we best be on our way." Sable announced. "Mogol, release him."

The other feathered creature strolled over to Griffin and grabbed a handful of green dust out of one of the undersized sacks hanging off his belt. Mogol sprinkled the abnormal dirt over the vines that bound Griffin so tightly. As if poisoned, the vines immediately withered away. Staring at his freed hands in wonderment, Griffin exclaimed, "Whoa."

"Now let's go, kid!" Mogol demanded.

"Wait!" cried Griffin.

"What is it, boy?" Sable's eyes were filled with anxiety.

Griffin had almost forgotten about John. He had to somehow let John know that he was going away. After all that John had given him, it just wouldn't be right to depart without any notice. "There is something I need to do first."

"What might that be?" Mogol asked.

"I have to say good–bye to someone." Griffin dug his fingers through his pockets and found a receipt and a dull pencil. He started to scribble words. "I just got to write someone a letter. Then we can be off."

"A letter to whom?" Sable was beginning to become impatient.

Griffin paused. "Umm ... a friend.

Rethinking what he had just said, Griffin realized that John was much more than a friend to him. John was a mentor, a father figure, and Griffin surely looked up to him. Saying his farewell to John would not sit well with Griffin. John was the only thing pulling him back from leaving home, but if his crazed father wasn't going to allow Griffin to attend John's lessons anymore, he would have no reason to stay. A few minutes later the letter was complete. It read:

John,

You have done more for me than you can ever imagine. I think I have found what I have been in search of, and I feel I need to take this chance. Your words of wisdom will be racing through my mind, and I know they will lead me to good fortune. I cannot be sure, but if we don't cross paths again, I want you to know you have been a father to me. And I thank you for that.

—Griff

After some convincing, the two beings allowed Griffin to drop the letter off at John's house. Sable stated, "Mogol will fly behind you to your visit to John's house. So if you stray, we will surely know." To be sure that they would be seeing Griffin again, Sable and Mogol kept Griffin's weapons until he returned.

The boy knew these woods like the back of his hand, and he ran along a path that would quickly take him to John's. Making it to the house in a short amount of time, Griffin quietly stepped onto the porch. Before slipping the note under the welcome mat, the boy waited and listened. He could hear John talking to his wife and rustling about the house. Griffin longed to talk to him, but he knew he couldn't explain everything with the amount of time he had. He slid the letter under the mat, leaving a corner of the paper exposed. Running back to the creatures, Griffin was quite happy that he wouldn't be going home to his father.

WATERFALL

When he reached Sable and Mogol, they started making their way through the woods. Getting his bow and quiver back, Griffin asked, "So, what are you guys exactly?"

"We are Critins, rulers of the skies," Sable replied.

"So if you guys are rulers of the skies, why are we walking? Or can the both of you not carry me?" Griffin slyly questioned.

"If you were but a few years younger, we could carry you." Sable was leading them through a vague path in the woods.

"Or but a few pounds lighter." Mogol chuckled, trailing behind the two of them.

Griffin turned back and scowled at Mogol. "So, Sable, why is that diamond so valuable?"

Taking the diamond in his claws, Sable explained, "You see this diamond? This here gem holds the life and death of us Critins. You see, boy, this is the key to our salvation."

"I'm not quite sure I follow, Sable."

"All right, boy. What would happen to your kind without the rich sunlight?"

"Well…everything would get real cold— and we would die."

"Well, this is our sun, and without it, we would die also. When the light dies in this jewel, we die as well. That's why Mogol and I are to be the guardians of the diamond. If it fell into the hands of the Shriekian, we would be no more."

Griffin kicked a small rock out of his path. "What and who exactly are the Shriekian? Why do they want to hurt you?"

"Griffin, of your land, who is the dominant species? Humans, am I correct?"

"Yeah."

"In our land of Aranwea, the Critins and the Shriekian are the two dominant races."

Nodding his head in approval, Mogol added, "Yes, and when two dominant species live in the same land, races will collide."

Spreading his feathered arms out, Sable explained, "We have no problem coexisting with them, but they think otherwise. Compared to the Shriekian, we think, act, and live the exact opposite from them."

"They are foul beings." Mogol started in. "They would love nothing more than to wipe our kind from existence, making them the only rulers of Aranwea. This is why we must not cower. We must stand up for all Critins and battle!"

"No! No! No!" Sable roared while firmly stopping. "There will be no battles! There will be no Critin blood shed on my behalf!"

Mogol's catlike eyes penetrated Sable. "If we sit...and take no action, they will come. All hope will be lost, and that *will* be on your behalf."

"You remember your place, and I'll do the same," Sable snapped as they started to follow the overgrown path once again.

The silence was broken when Griffin asked, "There was another? I... I mean another human brought to your land?"

Taking in some air, Sable explained, "Yes, yes, there was, and remembering how horribly that incident ended makes me wonder what we are doing with you."

Griffin reluctantly asked, "So, what happened to him?"

"Well, *she* went mad! Straight out of her mind she went! Humans are not from our world. Being there for as long as she had was more than a mind could adapt to. Her madness drove her to them... the Shriekian... and God knows what horrific death they bestowed upon her." Mogol ended with a shudder.

Griffin cried, "So that's what is gonna happen to me?"

"Well, we didn't start to see these changes in Adria until three years of being with us. You have a great while before you'll have to worry about that," Sable explained.

Griffin looked to the ground as if trying to solve an impossible mystery. "Did you say Adria?"

"Yes. Why do you question this?" Sable cocked his head to one side.

Griffin sighed, knowing the name sounded familiar. "Oh never mind," he said, thinking it must be a coincidence. "Where do these ... how do you say ... disturbed beings live?"

"The Shriekian live on the other end of Aranwea past the Roggon Woods. They linger in their murky depths and guard their domain, the Shriekian Domain," answered Mogol.

"They live in water? That's where they live?" Griffin asked.

"Precisely, we are the rulers of the sky; they are the rulers of the water. Land was meant for both of us Critins and Shriekian, but they want land and all of Aranwea to be owned by their kind ... and their kind only."

Walking deeper into the forest, Griffin could feel a cool breeze briskly patting his cheeks.

Griffin was at peace. He was not at peace because he was lingering in the woods that he so thoroughly enjoyed but because he felt he was doing something he was meant to do.

Looking through the vast thick trees, the boy asked, "So where are we going? I–I mean, I know we're going to Aranwea, but how are we getting there?"

"You sure ask a bundle of questions for a human," Mogol said, dissatisfied. "We are going to the waterfall."

Chuckling, Griffin spouted, "Are you serious? The only water source you will find back here is a lousy stream, and this stream couldn't even water a mouse. There's no waterfall here."

"And you are certain you are not mistaken?" Sable asked.

"Of course, I have known this forest my whole life. There is no waterfall."

The three of them stopped as they approached the stream Griffin had spoken of. The meager creek was about a foot wide and had a slight water flow. Griffin exclaimed, "I don't know what you consider a waterfall in Aranwea, but here in Oregon, this is anything but one."

"Shhhhh!" Mogol snapped.

At the tiny water's edge stood Sable. His beak was pointing to the heavens, and his feathered arms were stretched to the skies. Then silence— complete and utter silence. Griffin could hear neither the wind whispering through trees nor the cry of a song bird. Sable unfolded his wings as if to take flight.

Not a moment later, clouds began to form, and as if the sky had suffered a terrible loss, it started to rain. Heavy raindrops burst into many when touching the forest floor. Griffin had never laid eyes on such a sight. He could not see Sable, Mogol, or his hand before his face, for the rain was a continuous water flow.

Just as rapidly as it was brought on, the rain subsided, and the cloud cover disappeared. What once was a seemingly useless stream now was a rapid river. Shaking off some water, Sable grabbed a small whistle the size of a rubber band from his belt of tools.

"Ready for our ticket to your waterfall, Griffin?" Sable asked.

Griffin said nothing but stood next to Sable on the river's edge. He didn't know what to say, for he was in a state of disbelief of what had just taken place. Sable then placed the whistle in his mouth and kneeled down next to the edge of the river, placing the other half in the water. The feathered being sent a high–pitched sound throughout the water, sending the noise through the roaring river. "Wha … what are you doing?" Griffin stuttered.

"Just wait. These humans are always so impatient," Mogol said, shaking his head from left to right.

In an instant, something approached swiftly in the water. The mystifying object was undoubtedly a great size, for its force was ripping through the river, causing ten feet of water to spray up uncontrollably. Immediately before reaching the three of them, the object sunk into the depths of the river. The water went back to a flowing river until a creature emerged. First out of the water came a long, black, and outstretched head and neck. As it rose from the deep blue, Griffin could observe its back, which was consumed with a darkened green turtle–like shell. Protruding from the shiny belly of the beast were four pointed fins made perfectly for cutting through the river. The water beast also contained a stubby tail and black rubbery skin that served as a flaw-less way to glide through water with ease. Its mouth bared a set of deathly sharp fangs, but its eyes were not frightening. The neck alone was about fifteen feet tall, and the shell was the size of a small car.

"Griffin, meet Golydon; Golydon, meet Griffin. Now we best be on our way."

Griffin froze. "Don't…don't tell me we are riding that…that monster!"

"Unless you want to be swimming to the waterfall, I guess so. He won't bite; hop on and get a firm grip." The animal let out a shrill, ear–piercing shriek. "We're coming, Golydon! Just hold on!" Mogol demanded to the oversized beast.

Griffin walked toward the water creature. It lifted its left fin out of the water and slapped it on the ground before Griffin. This served as an ideal bridge. With much hesitation, Griffin cautiously walked across the slippery fin and onto the shell. Trailing closely behind him was Sable and Mogol. Getting on the solid shell, Sable warned, "Secure yourself, boy; you're in for a ride."

To make sure he wouldn't be losing the weapon that had saved his life, the boy slid his two bows up to his shoulder and tightened his quiver's straps. Lying down, Sable and Mogol dug their claws into the pentagonal–shaped crevices imbedded in the creature's shell. Griffin looked over at the two of them and quickly did the same. "Why do we have to lie down like this? Is the ride really going to be that bad?" Griffin asked. These words had only just escaped his mouth before the mighty animal had taken off just skimming the surface of the water. It took every ounce of strength in Griffin's body to keep him from flying off into the blue abyss. It was a greater task for Griffin to hang on, for he didn't have razor–sharp talons to tighten his loose grip.

The water creature cut through the river like a saw on wood. They were traveling at such a high velocity that when Griffin looked to the side he could only see a blur of green. Griffin's grip was slowly weakening. The river wound left and right, throwing Griffin side to side. "Slow down!" the distressed boy cried. But the force of the airflow clouded Sable and Mogol's hearing. He couldn't hang on much longer. *Is this where my journey will end?* Griffin thought. Grasping on to the prehistoric shell with only one hand now, he was struck with an idea. Reaching around ever so carefully, Griffin pulled out an arrow from his quiver. He thrust the arrow in the shell of the beast, just missing the soft flesh beneath. Grasping the arrow with both hands now, it was much easier for Griffin to stay on the wild animal. The beast started to slow down, and Griffin saw a drop–off with a large body of water spilling over it. They were on top of the waterfall. Golydon swam over to the bank and let them off.

Getting off the beast, the three of them were but ten feet away from the ledge. Griffin let out a sigh of relief, and his heart started to go back to its normal steady beat. "Thank you, Golydon," Mogol said, nodding his head. The beast let out another earth–shaking roar then sank into the river, leaving little bubbles on the surface.

Griffin followed the two of them to the very top edge of the collapsing water. Griffin was in true amazement. He had never seen a water-fall even remotely of this size. The thousands of gallons being tossed over the cliff's edge had Griffin fascinated. "How's that for a waterfall, Griffin?" Sable had his wings spread, present-ing the waterfall.

"Ahh, it's pretty cool I guess." Griffin didn't want to admit how impressed he actually was.

"We best not waste time. We still have quite a journey before we reach Aranwea. We must press on." Sable then pointed off to the left of the bank. There was a mossy stairway that arched down to the bottom of the waterfall. "We'll see you at the bottom!" The two of them became airborne, causing wind to swirl and rustle Griffin's hair about. The creatures then tucked their wings into their birdlike bodies and took a nosedive down the edge, staying in perfect alignment with the vertical water.

Griffin turned toward the green–covered steps and started the slippery path down. On the way down, he began to have second thoughts about this newfound journey.

THE SLAUGHTER

The stairway he followed wound to the bottom of the falls, an endless corkscrew. Taking each step with caution, Griffin wondered if he was making the right decision. He worried, *What if my letter was blown away and John never saw it?* Images of search and rescue teams investigating his disappearance entertained his every thought. He could just see his father being taken away in handcuffs as a suspect and his mother just sitting, taking it all in, wanting and needing to know what was going on. However, these ideas did not disturb him, for the thought of John not knowing what happened to him caused Griffin his only regret.

Pursuing the infinite descent, he tried to brush those possibilities away, for he very well knew he couldn't turn back even if he desired it. The steps came to an end, and he stood at the river's shoreline. The scenery was breathtaking. The air was pure, and it felt good to breathe it into his lungs.

"Come now." Standing unexpectedly behind him was Mogol. Startled, Griffin quickly turned around and nearly tripped into the clear water. "This way." Regaining his senses, Griffin followed Mogol onto an exceptionally narrow path. However, this path they followed was not ordinary, for it led into the middle of the river. It was nothing more than a bridge of rocks guiding them.

The end of the walkway led them to a circular island. Sable stood entirely concentrated on what was laid before him at the edge of the dirt island. He was facing the waterfall, which was about thirty feet away. It looked as though the mighty falls would swallow the meager island in one gulp. As Mogol and Griffin approached him, he began to sing a peaceful tune. Sable spoke in a language that Griffin's ears had never encountered. It was smooth and soft and got louder by the second. Moments later Griffin could hear nothing other than the music that came from Sable. Not even the gigantic crashing of the waterfall could make its way to his ears. It consumed his mind as he stood awestruck listening to the stunning sound. Sable stopped the pleasing song, and then something happened that Griffin could truly not fathom even in his wildest dreams. The continuous waterfall parted to each side as if cut down the middle by a powerful blade. A new path was born.

Suddenly emerging from the water was another rock bridge leading straight into the opening of the waterfall. "Right this way." Mogol placed his hand on Griffin's back, escorting him onto the newly revealed path. The mist of the falls fell to their faces as they neared the black entrance. Before entering the unknown, Sable exclaimed, "Hope you're not afraid of the dark."

The waterfall immediately shut as they entered. "W–where are we?" Griffin stammered. "I don't know about you guys, but humans can't see in the dark!" Griffin was sightless in the unknown place. He could only see the diamond shining about Sable's neck. To comfort himself, he got his shortbow and an arrow ready. As fear filled his mind, whispers sounded throughout the area. Moving his talons around the diamond, Sable made it brighten, causing light to illuminate throughout what appeared to be a cave.

Sable looked to Griffin, who seemed as though he was ready for battle. "Good. It is always intelligent to have a weapon ready in a place such as this," Sable stated and then cautiously moved forward.

As Mogol and Griffin followed the diamond carrier deeper into the damp cave, Mogol explained, "This place holds a horrible memory, a memory that is so dark and cold that all Critins shutter when speaking of it."

Bow still in hand, Griffin asked, "What happened? The Shriekian and you, did you battle here?"

"There was no battle. Torture is what took place here."

"What? Torture?" Griffin gasped.

"Many summers ago, before I was even brought into this land, the hatred between Critins and Shriekian was unleashed. You see..." Mogol paused. "It is hard to believe, but the Critins and Shriekian race used to live in harmony. This was until the night of the storm."

"So what does a storm have to do with torture?"

As they walked through the tunnel, Griffin intently watched for any sign of unknown movement. Every few moments the boy glanced behind him.

"Now, Griffin, this wasn't just *any* kind of storm. This was a storm to put all storms to shame. The Shriekian claimed to know a place where the storm could not pursue, a place of shelter and safety."

"And the shelter is this cave, right?"

"Precisely, so our kind followed the Shriekian to this place. Blinded from seeing their fate, they followed them deeper into this cave. Lightning struck the trees, and thunder sounded throughout Aranwea. Then, when they seemed to have all Critins cornered, they…attacked. All Shriekians bared their once–hidden weapons and slaughtered our kind. Those beings are pure evil. No mercy was to be had in them. Before I die I will have vengeance."

"But…" Griffin began. "If they slaughtered all Critins, then how are you two here?"

"I don't recall saying that *all* Critins were so foolish to believe their wicked ambush. One stood up to the rest; he didn't trust the Shriekian," Mogol said as he trailed closely behind Griffin.

"My father," Sable said.

"It was your father who saved the Critin race?" Griffin asked with much excitement.

Nodding his head, Sable continued. "Grathor was my father's name. He did not trust the Shriekian's ways. He took forty faithful Critins to the valley of Aranwea to wait out the storm. Once the storm had subsided, my father came to the knowledge of the massacre. Knowing that the remaining Critins would be safe, he went to this cave. What he found here you could not even imagine in your most gruesome dreams. He was never the same again. From that time forth my father vowed to regain the losses that the Critin race suffered. That is why I must carry on my father's will to protect our kind."

A crisp breeze rushed through the cave, and Griffin noticed a speckle of light leading out. "If you don't mind me asking, Sable, why don't you try and fight back?"

"Save that question for another day. Now come. We are nearing the end of the cave."

Curiosity overwhelmed Griffin, and he pressed on, "But I just don't get it. I mean … form an army. Find the Shriekian weakness!"

Sable pulled out the same dagger that had threatened Griffin before. He thrust the knife centimeters from Griffin's neck. "Enough, boy!"

"Sable! Stop! He didn't know!" Mogol protested.

Sable's feathered chest was moving up and down rapidly. The angered being lowered his blade away from Griffin's vulnerable neck and proceeded to the speckle of light. "S–S–Sable, I'm sorry, I didn't realize…" Griffin clenched his teeth in regret.

"That's enough, Griffin. Just let him be," Mogol suggested while the two of them once again trailed after Sable.

Long stalactites scowled at them as the light to the outside became brighter. Even though he nearly got knifed for being too inquisitive, Griffin still couldn't help his need to know what was bothering Sable. He speculated, *Maybe he's just scared or afraid to make the wrong decision.*

They stood before the end of the cave, and Griffin could see a blue sky overhead. The three of them stepped out of the dreary cave, and Griffin put his bow away. "Welcome to Aranwea," Sable announced.

The land that was laid before them possessed pure and natural beauty. Hills of green engulfed the land as far as Griffin could see. White clouds hovered in the sky, and water spilled through a stream throughout a nearby forest. Being the outdoorsmen that he was, Griffin regarded the scenery with a great deal of appreciation. Remarkably divine and untouched was this place. "Now come along. The village is not far." Sable was again leading the way, and they followed him deep into the nearby woods.

It took Griffin some time to get used to the thick shrubbery, for this forest was much denser than his back home. There were giant redwood trees planted about the woods. The redwoods' sizes were so mighty that they must have been birthed before Christ, and their length seemed to reach to the stars.

As the boy and the two feathered beings walked through the lively forest, Griffin wondered many things. He did not ask them, for he didn't want to be reintroduced to Sable's blade for the third time. *Would it be a small or large village? What are their houses like? And how are the villagers going to feel about another human being brought to their land?*

Hoping this question wouldn't get him into too much trouble, Griffin reluctantly asked, "Are we almost there?"

"Nearly," Sable replied.

"You know, boy, this would be a much easier journey if you could fly," Mogol complained.

Griffin rolled his eyes. "You know, you're completely right. Please excuse me while I go sprout a pair of wings; it'll only take a second."

"Enough, you two," Sable interrupted. "We're here."

LEADER OF ALL CRITINS

Looking down from the green hill on which they stood, Griffin could see a village teeming with life. Many Critins moved busily about the village. Some were flying, and some walked around on two feet. One could hear the soft tune of a Critin playing an instrument similar to the whistle Sable had. There were little huts made of stone. The huts were lean and sturdy and held no doors, only an opening where a door should be. At the end of the numerous stone huts rested a mountain of boulders that rose high into the air. When the clouds cleared from the mountainous pile of rocks, something magnificent came into view. A pristine and untouchable castle sat atop the rocky mound.

The gray castle walls reached many feet into the sky, and white clouds floated around them. Jetting out farther into the sky were several towers.

Griffin gasped. "Unbelievable. Whoever lives there has it made!"

Taking a horn from his belt, Mogol blew on it, echoing a deep sound throughout the town. All Critins stopped immediately what they were doing. "He's back!" Many of them shouted. The villagers then formed two single–file lines leading up to the castle. "Don't stray, Griffin," Sable ordered.

They hiked down the grassy hill and began walking through the middle of the lined up Critins. There was a murmur of restless chatter about the villagers. Many of them gasped with disapproval at the sight of this human. "You are mad, Sable! You're crazy to bring another human to our land!" one angry Critin shouted.

Ignoring the fuming villager, Sable announced, "All questions shall be answered at the Oval at sundown!"

The confused beings scattered, and the three of them continued walking toward the castle. "I don't think they're too excited to see me," the boy said sarcastically.

"They'll learn to like you." Sable turned toward Griffin. "You can't really blame them for their distastefulness for humans though."

"Yes," Mogol added. "Humans in our past haven't exactly been the most fortunate thing to our kind."

What could this person have done to bring so much hate to the humans? Griffin pondered to himself as they walked past the stone buildings. Beaked faces peered out of the huts as Griffin walked past. Griffin felt vulnerable and unwanted. "So...where are we going now?" the boy asked.

Pointing his sharp talon ahead of them, Sable explained, "Your answer lies straight ahead."

Gazing before him, Griffin looked upon the gigantic boulders and the majestic castle that was perched on top. "Up there? Let me guess, we're going to see the leader ... or king and let him know the diamond is safe?"

Mogol looked to Sable as if longing to tell a secret of great importance. Sable paused then explained, "Griffin, only the leader of all Critins can obtain this diamond."

Griffin had a confused look on his face. Then his eyes lit up, and he exclaimed, "But ... but that would make you ... Sable? You're the leader of your land!"

Nodding his feathered head, he replied, "Yes ... yes, Griffin. I am the bearer of the diamond as I am the leader of all Critins."

Griffin ran his right hand through his black ruffled hair and cried, "Why did you fail to mention this in the first place? Or did you just completely forget? And you, Mogol, are you something unusual that I should know about also, maybe some kind of dark sage?"

"Actually, I'm a dust keeper," Mogol retorted.

"Great, great. Well, it looks like I'm the only truthful one here."

"Don't you mouth a word about being truth-ful. You very well know you never asked us who we were, only what we were," Sable countered as he continued leading the way to the castle.

"Well, it seems you could have told me something that important," the displeased boy protested.

Approaching the bottom of the rock basin, Mogol unfolded his wings, ruffled his feathers a bit, and said, "We'll send a ride down for you, unless you would rather climb of course."

"Depends on what form my ride comes in." Griffin was remembering the last journey he had with Golydon.

The two of them took flight, and Sable shouted back, "Just wait there, Griffin! We'll meet you at the top!"

Watching them shrink as they rose higher, Griffin still couldn't believe that Sable was the leader of the Critin race. "The leader of this place...with a castle...needs my help," Griffin said, surprised.

Deep in thought, the pleased boy didn't realize his ride to Sable's castle was near him.

"Hello," an unknown voice from behind said. Griffin spun around quickly to acknowledge where the voice came from. He gasped at what his eyes had landed on and stumbled backward, falling to the soft dirt.

"You're a … you're a … dragon!" the startled boy exclaimed from the spot he fell.

"Yes, I'm Snolon, and might I know your name, sir?" The soft tone of her voice gave off a reassuring feeling. Its sharp, spiked tail stretched almost to the length of its body. The dragon's stout legs stood unmovable on the soil. Sunlight reflected off the dragon's white scales, giving it an angel–like glow. Her wings were tucked securely back as she sat on all fours.

"My name's Griffin," he told her, picking himself up off the ground.

"Pleased to make your acquaintance, Griffin." The dragon's jagged teeth appeared when she spoke.

"The pleasure is all mine. It's not every day that a guy like me gets to meet a dragon."

"Well, I'll probably be the last you meet too, Griffin. There aren't many of my kind left in this land! Hop on my back, and I'll take you to the castle doors, if you would like."

Looking up at the vertical slope, Griffin said, "A ride would be great."

Kneeling her two front legs down, Griffin made his way toward her. Using the dragon's neck for support, he hopped on her and secured his bows and quiver. "Ready, Griffin?" she asked.

Griffin wrapped his arms around Snolon's neck. "As ready as I'm going to be!" he cried.

"Then let's go! We don't want to keep Sable waiting!"

As soon as these words had fled her mouth, they were gone. The dragon's outstretched wings cut through the air sending them spiraling upward at a very high velocity. Griffin had to fully embrace Snolon's neck to keep from falling to his death.

Reaching the castle in seconds, Snolon kneeled once again and let him off. Griffin appeared quite flustered. "Thank you ... Snolon."

Before she left his presence, Snolon turned her lengthy neck around and reminded, "If you ever want to get more familiar with the skies, I'm always here."

"Always?" he speculated.

"Yes, Griffin. I'm here to protect the castle. That is my duty," the dragon replied.

"Ah, Snolon, thank you for bringing Griffin here so promptly. Come now, Griffin," Sable said as he drew nearer to them.

Leaving the dragon, Sable and Griffin approached the two castle doors. They were tall and wide and appeared to be made for a family of giants. Sable pushed them open, and they stepped inside.

The fortress within was almost as extraordinary as the outside. Entering the building, Griffin could see a spiraling staircase leading up to many levels of the castle. The ceilings were endless and unreachable. Throughout the castle, many paintings hung. Each painting was of a different feathered being with the red diamond hanging around the blackened part on its chest. Griffin followed Sable down the hallway where the canvases hung. "These paintings of Critins…are they family?" Griffin asked as he gazed at each intently.

"They are the royal family of the stone, as they are my family. Just like me, they all were sworn to protect the diamond at all costs," Sable replied. They trailed through the darkened hallway. It was the kind of hallway one would see in daunting films—never ending it was. "Here we are." Sable stopped at one of the hallway doors. Placing his clawed hand around the doorknob, Sable thrust it open. As the door slid open, dust particles fell from above, causing Griffin to sneeze profusely.

Covering his mouth, the boy coughed. "Well, I see this room has been used recently."

"If it doesn't suit your needs, there's always room outside with the dragon," Sable replied.

Stepping inside of his new home, Griffin replied, "No, no, this will be fine. I already feel at home!"

"Perfect! Now get acquainted, and I will call for you when the meeting is near."

The undersized room held nothing but a wooden bed, a large stained–glass window, and a petite table made of wood. The area was small and plain, but Griffin didn't care. He walked over to the window and tugged on its hinges. The opened window allowed Griffin to see for miles. The Critin village and the forest they came out of were in his sight. The beauty of the land had him mesmerized.

To keep the chill from pursuing him, Griffin gently shut the colorful stained–glass window. Taking a seat on the shaky bed, he freed himself of his two bows and quiver full of arrows. Fixing his eyes on his shortbow, Griffin sighed. "What have a got myself into, John?"

TRUSTLESS

His stomach growled at him, allowing Griffin to know just how hungry he was. It was now late in the evening, and the boy hadn't had a gulp of food since the snack with John the day prior.

"Griffin!" Sable appeared at the doorway. "Throw this on. It gets a bit cold at the Oval." Sable tossed him a long black robe with a triangular hood. "You will be receiving an impressive wardrobe later, but for now we must be off."

Slipping into the dark cloak, Griffin scanned himself and said, "Thanks."

"Yes, now follow me. Oh, and bring your bow and a single arrow as well," Sable stated, exiting room.

Griffin grabbed his shortbow and an arrow and began to follow Sable into the hallway.

"Where's this Oval at?" the curious boy asked.

"The roof," Sable replied. "And before we get there, there's something you must have knowledge of."

"And that would be?" Griffin was gawking at the many portraits again.

"You know that girl that I spoke of earlier? She is the reason why my people look in dismay toward the human kind."

"But…what did she do to cause so much hatred?"

"Adria was her name, and she handed the Shriekian the key to our life. She gave them the knowledge of our weakness. They have been after the diamond to this day. The Shriekian invade our village regularly to slaughter whoever stands in their path."

"I don't get it." Griffin was lightly tossing his head from left to right. "Was she not trustworthy? Well, she obviously wasn't trustworthy, so why did you trust her?"

"As I told you earlier, Griffin, being in Aranwea does something to your kind. After being in our land for as long as she was, it finally got the best of her. They were calling for her for quite some time, and she finally went to them."

"So, it wasn't her fault then ... right, Sable?"

Sable paused as if unsure what his answer was. "I see it as no fault on her, but the rest of my people see her as nothing more than a betrayer."

They stopped at the bottom of the spiral staircase. "Betrayer?" Griffin had a stunned expression. "But she didn't mean to do what she did."

"She didn't mean to, but Adria got blamed nonetheless. Now the meeting will be held just beyond this stairway."

The stairway wound higher and higher, and Griffin worried the end of them would never come. As he walked in upward circles, Griffin still couldn't understand the Critins' disgust for Adria; after all, she couldn't help what she had done. The boy pondered how the Shriekian must have put an end to her life. He shuddered at the thought of this.

His prayers were answered; Griffin and Sable had reached the top. They stood at the entrance of a small door with feathers made of gold clinging to it. Before opening the door, Sable explained, "Just let me do the talking, okay?" Griffin gave Sable a quick nod, and Sable opened the door. "Welcome to the Oval."

The castle top had an egg–shaped surface. The roof was enclosed on all sides with a thick wall that was severely chipped. The castle was undeniably of great age. The side walls reached just below Griffin's broad shoulders. White clouds drifted into sight, preventing an amazing view of the landscape.

"So…where are the villagers? It is sundown. Did I really scare them off earlier?" the boy joked.

"They'll come." Sable's voice was filled with certainty.

In an instant, the sound of hundreds of working wings came into their hearing. The whole village flocked to the Oval in moments.

Old Critins, middle–aged Critins, and young Critins came together to hear what Sable had to declare. White, catlike eyes peered at Griffin as they assembled a semicircle around Sable and the boy.

"My fellow Critins!" Sable stretched his arms upward as he shouted. "As you see the diamond is once again safe and untouched! Our race is still strong and prosperous! I am not going to deny that our enemy is gaining strength. For this very reason, I have brought this boy to our land!"

"You might as well hand them the diamond yourself! The humankind cannot be trusted!" An angry village dweller snarled.

Many of them nodded their feathered heads in approval to this fuming Critin. "Yes! I too had these same visions slip into my thoughts, but when Griffin's true value became vivid I realized something. I realized that coming across another human was a pure blessing!" Sable paused.

"Yeah! Just like Adria! She was a *sure* blessing!" a voice in the uneasy sea of beings bellowed.

Many of the Critins' eyes were fixed on Griffin in disgust. They boy's heart pounded out of control, and his hands grew hot and sweaty; Griffin felt out of place and helpless. Mogol was pushing through the crowd and hollered, "Adria and Griffin are far from the same person! This boy who stands before us is stronger than she! And this boy comes with new artillery that no one can defy."

Sable started again, "Yes, he speaks the truth!" Sable turned toward Griffin. "Reveal your weapon."

Griffin cautiously slid his shortbow and the razor–sharp arrow from under his black cloak. Some of the Critins gasped at the sight of the unfamiliar craft.

Feeling a jolt of confidence with the weapon in his palm, Griffin began to speak. "Critins of Aranwea! Hear Sable and Mogol! I am not your enemy, and I will do whatever I can to keep your diamond safe!"

A deranged Critin burst through the crowd after Griffin. "You will do nothing of the sort, stupid human!" The villager sneered.

Sable, predicting the act, glided in front of Griffin. He spread his wings out wide to keep the being from getting to Griffin.

Trying to stop himself from penetrating Sable, the angry Critin's talons screeched on the cement, leaving scratch marks embedded in the castle top. He came to an abrupt halt before slamming into the diamond barrier.

Sticking his finger out at the enraged villager, Sable said, "Don't you charge once more! Now step back before I have you banished!"

Griffin stood behind Sable speechless and frozen as the insane villager rose to his feet. "The meeting is over! You all may return home!" Sable called out.

As they all flocked away, Sable turned to Griffin and said in disappointment, "Now you see why I wanted to do all the talking."

HER WORDS

Back at his room, Griffin sat on the hard bed with his head sagging and arms folded. He was ashamed that he had spoken out of line after Sable asked him not to. The boy didn't know how to make things right, but he knew one thing for certain—he owed Sable a sincere apology.

"Not bad for your first night. If I do remember right, it wasn't until her fourth night our last human got into a quarrel with a villager." Mogol stood in the doorway with a candle in one hand and a plate holding food, and a cup of water in the other.

Griffin looked to him in dismay. "I suppose you have come to cheer me up?"

"Listen, Griffin, it wasn't the wisest choice you could have made, but all hope for gaining their trust is not lost."

"I–I just don't understand! Sable brought me to this place knowing his people wouldn't approve of me, right?"

"Precisely."

"Then why am I here? I'm turning his people against him!

"Because, Griffin, Sable sees something in you, strength, courage and most of all loyalty, and I feel the same as he."

"Well, I sure proved that statement to be true tonight, now didn't I?" Griffin's voice shook with shame.

Resting the plate and candle on the small table, Mogol explained, "What's taken place is something that you cannot change. So, boy, let us make what is yet to come something that you will have no desire to change."

Griffin nodded his head. Exiting the room, Mogol said, "You best be get fed and rested and remember tomorrow is a day anew."

Griffin grabbed the plate of food and set it at his thighs. Sitting on the bed, he drank some water and began to examine his meal. It appeared to be some type of exotic fish, for vibrant turquoise scales clung to it. The meat was still warm, and the boy began to remember how hungry he was. The fish meat was soft and contained no bones. Griffin consumed the meat down to its last scale and the water down to its last drop.

Tiredness overcame him. He kicked off his black sneakers and tossed the cloak on the table chair. As he laid his head down on the thin pillow, Griffin noticed a discomfort. "Stupid pillow!" he said under his breath. "This thing's probably older than that stupid red diamond!" He sat up on his knees and punched the pillow in hopes to make it softer. The blow to the pillow made a loud thump and caused pain to overwhelm his closed fist. "Ouch!" Griffin yelped while holding his throbbing hand with the other. Griffin lifted up the pillow, revealing a hard–covered journal. Picking it up, he gawked at it in confusion. He opened it to page one. It read:

My name is Adria Heprum. I ran away from where some would call my home. I don't call that horrible place my home. Here is where I'm meant to be. Here with the Critins is where I belong. They are my true friends and family that I never had but always wanted. The Critins are a part of me, as I am a part of them. They treat me no differently then they treat each other, and I adore them for this.

I have been living with the Critins for about three years now. It is my birthday today, May 16th, which is why Sable has very graciously given me this journal. Sable is the one who carries the diamond, and he is my favorite of them all. I also like Mogol. Although he gives me a hard time, he means well. I have grown so close to all of them. I have never been filled with so much love. I never want to leave.

The page ended. "Adria Heprum," Griffin whispered out loud. That sounded dreadfully familiar to the boy, but he could not quite recall where it came from. *It seems like she writes about a completely different race,* Griffin thought.

These creatures that Adria wrote of were kind and loving, unlike the beings that had shown so much hatred toward Griffin today.

He turned the page, hoping to find more information.

May 17

It is nighttime, and I'm sipping on a bowl of hot herbal soup. I'm not feeling myself today. I fear I am catching a cold. So I must rest. There is not the medication here like in the human land so I must take extra precaution.

The next journal entry wasn't written until over a month later. Griffin read further.

June 25th, I am not feeling like I belong here. Though ... I don't feel like I should go back to where I came from. I'm scared. Ever since I became sick, whispers surround my thoughts. As the days pass by, I feel I am being dragged further into the unknown. I need someone. It is becoming harder to resist. They are tempting me.

And then there was no more. Griffin flipped through the remainder of the pages only to find they were unused. Her last words tugged at Griffin. *It is becoming harder to resist. They are tempting me.* These words alone sent a chill down his spine. Griffin tossed the journal under his bed. He pulled the two layers of brown and green covers over him and hesitantly blew the fire from the candle. Griffin found sleep, but his dreams were not pleasant.

A NEW ERA

"Awaken, Griffin!" a voice shouted. With a halo of tiredness hanging about his head, Griffin struggled to open his dreary eyes. After three attempts, the boy's eyes were finally able to fully open. Directly above his face was Sable's beak pointing downward. Startled, Griffin rose quickly, just missing contact with Sable's sharp bill. Drawing his feathered face back, Sable said, "Sorry to scare you, boy. Now meet me outside the castle as soon as you are available."

As Sable left the room, Griffin spoke to him. "Sable … I'm sorry about last night. I … "

"Just meet me outside the castle. What needs to be discussed will be discussed then," Sable interrupted, exiting the room.

Hitting his head back on the pillow, Griffin sighed. "Now you've done it, Griffin." He sat up and slipped on his shoes; he then left the room to seek out Sable.

Beyond the oversized doors, Sable was nowhere to be seen. The boy looked about the skies for him. Sable appeared to be nowhere. Griffin could see no life but only Snolon rapidly soaring in the direction of the castle.

The dragon swiftly made her landing directly before Griffin. She exclaimed, "Sable awaits your arrival." Snolon plummeted to the ground. Griffin found that clutching on to the dragon was much easier compared to the first time he had ridden on her.

They reached the ground where Sable stood, anticipating Griffin's company. Sliding off the beast's smooth scales, Griffin stood before Sable. "Thank you. You may take your leave, Snolon," Sable said to the dragon.

Tipping her head to Sable, she then departed to the sky. Griffin started, "Please forgive me for last night. I was out of line. Just don't send me home. I will never be able to forget about this place if you do." Griffin's eyes showed much hopefulness while waiting for his reply.

"You are going nowhere," Sable replied. He had not the anger in his voice that the boy had expected.

"I–I'm not?

"No." Sable began to walk, and Griffin followed.

Griffin and Sable trailed down the middle pathway of the village. As Griffin passed by, the villagers peeked their curious faces out of the stone huts.

Sable said nothing. They just kept trekking through the small town side by side. A wind was softly approaching from the east, and due to no cloud coverage, the castle was completely visible. The boy tried to imagine what was surrounding Sable's thoughts when the silence was broken. "Can you craft replicas of your weapon?" Sable asked.

Griffin looked to him in puzzlement. "What? More bows and arrows? But why?"

"I just need to know, boy. Is such a thing possible for you to do?"

"Well yeah, I mean with the right tools, yes, I could. Why, Sable?"

"And what is your weapon made of? Wood, yes...but what kind?"

"Umm...well, elm trees work great. That's what I usually use, but any wood that is bendable will work. Sable, what's all this about?"

Sable breathed in the refreshing air through his nostrils and began to explain, "Griffin, not a year ago I lost my son to the Shriekian. I lost him, my only son, Vector."

Then it struck Griffin. It all made complete sense now. Sable lost a loved one to them. If he tried to overpower the Shriekian, then more could be lost. "What? But how?" The boy questioned in astonishment.

Sable started. "We had gotten into an argument that same night. He wished to go to war with them. I was convinced that our kind was not strong enough to defeat them. Vector claimed that he would singlehandedly bring down this mighty race by finding their weakness. I, of course, would not allow him to do such a thing. I thought he had listened to me…" Sable paused and drew in much air. "Hours later news came to me that Vector was gone. I knew where he had gone, and I shuddered to think of it. As I opened the castle doors to seek out my son, Mogol stopped me. I frantically told him that I needed to find Vector when he handed me a linen bag. The bag had been sent down the river that flows from the Shriekian domain to ours. I knew the bag had been from Shriekian soil, for it smelt of their foul, marshy lands. I cautiously opened the bag." Griffin watched Sable intently as he spoke. "It was filled with my son's feathers."

Griffin walked along with Sable, not knowing what to say, not knowing how to react. The boy couldn't envision losing someone so close to him. Griffin felt a deep sorrow for Sable. "I had no idea. That must have been horrible for you!" Griffin exclaimed.

"Yes, it was a cruel and evil act, but no more tears shall be shed, and no more time shall be spent in sorrow. This is the very reason I questioned your bow–making skills, Griffin. A new era is about to arrive—an era where the Critin race will no longer live in fear, an era where I will follow out my son's wishes. We shall go to war."

"War?" Griffin gasped. "You are taking your kind to war?"

"Yes, and you will provide my soldiers with your human weapon. You, Griffin, you will teach them the skills that we need to defeat the Shriekian. You see, boy, my kind has never laid eyes on weapons such as yours, nor has the Shriekian. They will be greatly caught off guard." The boy stared at the ground, trying to gather all that was being asked of him. From the moment Griffin took his first steps, he knew he was different. He knew he was worth something of great importance. An urge buried deep inside of Griffin told him he was meant to do something extraordinary. That same urge was beginning to be revealed. He realized what he must do. He had to help this species live to see a day when fear wouldn't follow them. He had to lead the Critins to victory.

"Well, let's make your son proud." Griffin smiled at Sable.

Sable sent a smile back to him. "Yes, we shall make him proud! Now let us go back to the castle and fill our stomachs. Then we will announce to my people what we have just spoken of. Except this time, keep your mouth closed." Sable laughed.

Griffin nodded with reddened cheeks and agreed, "Fine by me."

Back at the castle, Sable led Griffin into the dining hall. The room was enormous and had a large, egg–shaped table in the center of it. The dining hall also had stained–glass windows that looked like those that were in Griffin's room. Griffin and Sable sat down at the table, which included a tablecloth that contained swirling shades of red. Mogol took a seat next to Sable. Fish was brought to each of them by a Critin who appeared to be the castle servant. Griffin's meal was different than Mogol's and Sable's. His was again cooked and sliced into bite–sized morsels. Mogol and Sable's fish was not cooked. Their fish looked as if they had just been fished out of the ocean only moments before, for they still had lifeless, open eyes. Using his fingers,

Griffin placed a piece of tender meat in his mouth and mumbled, "How'd you know I would like my fish cooked?"

Mogol swallowed the fish in one gulp and then said, "Remember you are not the first human that we have stumbled upon."

"Right, I always forget that."

When the meal had been finished, the same Critin who had brought them their food reappeared and took their dishes. As the servant obtained Griffin's plate, the boy said, "Thank you." But the only response given was a smug look. A little embarrassed, Griffin said under his breath, "Never mind then."

"There will be a meeting at the Oval tonight," Sable announced to Griffin and Mogol. "I'm going to let the villagers know of this. While I'm out, I'm sure Mogol wouldn't mind giving you a better tour of the castle. Sound good, Griff?"

Griff? the boy thought. The only person he allowed to call him Griff was John, but coming from Sable, it sounded just as likeable. Griffin said, "Yeah, sounds fine."

"Great," Sable replied. "Oh, and before I forget, Griffin, could I borrow your bow and a single arrow? I'm going to have our finest woodworker examine it."

"Yeah, I'll go get it." Griffin left the dining hall and was back with his shortbow and an arrow in moments. Griffin handed it to Sable.

"It won't be needed for long," Sable reassured.

Sable left their presence. "What's this meeting all about?" Mogol curiously asked Griffin.

"What? Sable hasn't told you?" Griffin replied.

"No, no words have left his mouth that were worthy to be said at the Oval."

What? I'm the only one who knows that war is coming? Griffin thought to himself. The boy was astonished that Sable had only told him. If even Mogol had no knowledge of the newly decided war, then surely no one else did. Griffin felt a large amount of pride to be the first to bear the news. "Ummm...well, I guess we'll all find out at the meeting. I'm not quite sure what this is all about either," Griffin lied. He didn't want Sable to be displeased if he were not supposed to speak of the information he contained.

Confused, Mogol replied, "Yeah … I assume so."

"So are you gonna show me the castle?

"Those were my orders. Right this way."

The castle was much larger than Griffin had anticipated. Mogol showed Griffin a few of the many rooms. "And this one is Sable's," Mogol announced while gesturing Griffin to a hallway door. As Mogol opened the door, they stepped inside. The ceiling was continuous, and the walls owned bright stained–glass windows that hung beautifully around them. The dorm was strangely empty. "So if this is Sable's room, then where does he sleep?" Griffin questioned while gazing around the area.

"Every night we Critins shed a lot—not all, but many of our feathers. And each night we make a nest with them. When sleeping, we gain new feathers fast. In the morning, we discard our old nest and make a new one at night," Mogol explained.

"Odd."

"Odd? No, I would say that sleeping on wooden rectangles as you humans do is odd." Mogol laughed, and they left Sable's room.

Not far from Sable's, they came upon another room. This place was just a bit smaller than the previous room. It contained a unique presence for many drawings and paintings clung to the walls. The paintings were genuine. Such detail was added to these drawings. One of the pieces of work presented what appeared to be Sable reaching out his hand with the red diamond. Each stroke of ink sat embedded in the paper without fault.

Griffin peered into the room. His eyes became fixed by one of the paintings. It pulled him into the room, followed by Mogol. Griffin viewed the image of Sable. "Who drew these?"

"That Vector was a talented young Critin." Mogol sighed while picking up a painting that was placed on a table.

"Vector, you mean Sable's son? This was his room?"

"Yes, yes, it was, and Sable's changed nothing in this room since he left us."

"And I don't plan on changing it," Sable announced, appearing in the doorway. He was holding Griffin's shortbow and arrow. His arms were crossed, and his eyes were dissatisfied.

Mogol and Griffin shifted their bodies toward the displeased Sable. "Oh, Sable, I was just showing Griffin here some of your son's impressive paintings," Mogol quickly explained. "Did you have success in telling the villagers of the meeting?"

"Yes, I had success in telling the villagers just as you have had success in invading my son's privacy. I said give him a better look at the castle. That does not entitle rummaging about my son's belongings." Sable's eyes were looking intently into Mogol's. "Here, Griffin." Sable held out his shortbow and arrow. Griffin took his belongings. "Now I expect to see you both at the Oval this evening. Until then." Sable exited through the doorway.

"Sorry, guess I should have warned you," Mogol apologized. "Sable's protective of this old room and everything it contains."

Mogol showed Griffin throughout the castle a bit more. When they were finished, Griffin took refuge in his room until the meeting began.

THEY WILL FALL

"My good Critins, fear will soon be nonexistent in our near future!" The meeting had just begun. Griffin stood next to Sable, and all the villagers' eyes again seemed to be fixed on him. The boy was not sure how the Critins would react to the idea of war. This worried Griffin.

"The Shriekian have compelled us to live in agony! They come time and time again seeking to destroy our precious diamond. Mogol and I are forced to retreat to safety when they come, leaving our few soldiers to protect our kind. Our numbers are rapidly depleting. No more shall we wait for them to pursue our village! No more shall we flee! With the Shriekian force growing stronger and our race growing weaker,

we must take action! War…is…inevitable."
Sable ended. He waited to hear the responses of
his people.

Endless gasps sounded through the Oval.
"War?" All beings were overwhelmed and
seemed not to know how to answer.

"With the Shriekian growing stronger, how
do you think we even have a hope to win this
war?" one voice in the crowd shouted.

"With a new breed of artillery, we shall
bring down this mighty race. This war will be
won if we bring to the battle a weapon that
the Shriekian has never laid eyes on. We will
greatly catch them off guard, and by the end
of this warfare no Shriekian will rest their eyes
upon a Critin without a shudder of fear!" Sable
roared to the uneasy crowd.

"And who shall provide us with a superior
weapon? It cannot be this…this *human*." Sepa-
rating the crowd was one of Sable's army lead-
ers. This Critin was a tough, rugged creature
with ruffled feathers. A scar passing through
his left eye down to his cheekbone made him
an easy being to recognize. "Do not tell me that

this meager boy is supposed to lead us to victory." His words were forceful and unforgiving. He glared at Griffin.

The unimpressed army leader approached Griffin. He settled but two feet from Griffin and growled, "Humans are weak, Sable. You should have realized that from the last encounter! If it wasn't for Adria Heprum, we wouldn't be living like savages! She and all humans will forever be hated by our kind! She has doomed us all."

Feeling his hand grip, Griffin shouted, "It wasn't her fault! You don't have a clue what she went through!"

"Enough!" Sable howled while stepping in between the two feuding beings. Sable grabbed the Critin's feathered neck and muttered to him, "Now listen here, Vetch. If you want to lead my army, you best do as I say. This boy has provided our kind with an upper hand. Now I know you want to claim ourselves a free race just as much as I." Sable released him.

Vetch looked to the ground for a bit. He then turned his eyes toward Griffin and said,

"This boy shall provide us with what we need, nothing more."

Staring back into Vetch's catlike eyes, Griffin realized this would not be the last feud they would share. "What are you looking at, boy?" Vetch mocked then took flight into the cloud–covered air.

Griffin loosened his grip. "The meeting is over. Go seek rest, knowing this is the dawn of a new era!" Sable shouted to all.

A whirlwind of flapping wings soon filled the air. Moments later all Critins retreated to their stone huts. Flying over to Griffin and Sable was Mogol. Excitedly Mogol exclaimed, "Yes! Sable, this is very wise of you! We will make the Shriekian pay! Mark my word!"

Ignoring Mogol, Sable turned to Griffin, "Are we going to go through this every meeting you attend?"

"I'm sorry, but he had it coming! Talking about Adria like that… it just isn't right." Griffin defended.

"Whether it is right or wrong, I cannot stick up for you every time, Griffin. No respect is to be had for someone who has to cower behind another, and when I said do not say a word I meant it."

"I didn't need your help if that is what you think. Gaining the respect of your people let alone him will take a miracle."

"Well I suggest you start looking for one because you will be teaching the army and him the ways of the bow very soon," Sable warned him.

Later that night Griffin lay in bed consumed by his thoughts. He thought about the hatred Vetch for him, how he missed John, and the mystery with Adria Heprum. His mind was racing, and although it was late, he had no desire for sleep.

GRIFFIN'S NIGHT FLIGHT

Griffin's occupied mind had at last come to ease. All was silent; all was calm. The boy lay moments away from slumber when a loud sound struck the window. Shocked, Griffin sprang out of bed and flopped on the hard floor. Quickly rising to his feet, he hastily said, "Who's out there?"

"Open the window, and you will see!" the unknown voice from outside replied.

"First you tell me who you are, and no lies!" the distraught boy bellowed. Griffin took his shortbow in hand and an arrow. He crept over to the window while setting up the arrow. The boy then unlatched the window and immediately pointed the arrow outside. Griffin found his weapon positioned straight at the nostrils of a large, airborne beast.

It was Snolan, the dragon guardian of the castle. Lowering his weapon, Griffin spoke in a whisper, "What the heck are you doing?"

Wings flapping effortlessly, she smiled. "I thought you might want to see the land from a better view tonight."

Confused, Griffin asked, "What are you talking about?"

Spinning around so that her back now faced Griffin, she said, "Get on, and I'll show you." Griffin stepped back and shook his head. "No, no, I can't just trust a dragon that shows up at my window in the middle of the night. The villagers … or … or Vetch probably sent you to kill me or something."

"I have no interest in harming you, Griffin. The Critins may not trust humans, but I think otherwise."

"No … I can't."

"Well, then I guess all humans aren't the same," Snolan remarked while facing Griffin once again. "She loved those night flights."

"Who are you talking…" But then he stopped, for he knew exactly who she was talking about. She was speaking of Adria. He pondered, *If she can do it, then so can I.* "Well, I guess a quick ride would be all right. A short ride is all. Then you'll bring me back here, right?" Griffin hesitated.

"Yes! Yes! Of course. Now get on, and find yourself a firm grip," Snolan excitedly replied, turning her back to him once more.

Griffin set his shortbow and arrow on the bed. He then cautiously stepped onto the dragon's scale–protected back. Wrapping his legs around Snolan's belly and his arms around her neck, Griffin exclaimed, "A quick ride is all!"

"As you wish!"

In an instant they were plummeting straight down the back side of the castle. As they made their descent, Snolan stayed but a hair away from the castle wall, almost grazing it at times.

Just before hitting the bottom, the dragon swiftly pulled back up and began to rise. They came to a steady pace, and Griffin stammered,

"I was definitely *not* ready for that! I almost threw up!"

Snolan laughed. "Well, good thing you didn't, or I would have dropped you myself!"

They were a boat on a peaceful sea. The air was crisp. Griffin released his grip on the dragon's neck. The land that lay under them was undisturbed. There were many stars out, and the boy gazed at them in serenity. He felt as if he could reach them with one stretch of his arm. As he felt the wind of the passing breeze, the boy could not even fathom what he was experiencing. Griffin at all times dreamed of something extraordinary happening to him, but something of this magnitude had him questioning if all this was reality. He felt free. Snolan flew them over hills of green with ease. They passed many large redwood trees that were almost the same height in which they were flying. The moon shone from above, shedding light on the land beneath them.

An hour passed, and Snolan sighed. "Well, best get you back to the castle."

As they made a round turn and headed in the direction of the castle, Griffin was hit with a question. "Snolan, where's the rest of your kind? I mean other dragons?"

"You're looking at her," she said.

"What? Wait, you mean you're the last of the dragons? But are you sure? What happened to the rest?" Griffin asked.

"I do not know what fate they encountered. All I remember is being lost and confused. That is until the Critins took me in."

"But how do you know for sure? They could be out there. Have you tried looking?"

"They are gone," Snolan interrupted.

They arrived back at the castle. Griffin hopped through his opened window and said, "Thanks for the ride, Snolan. I would love to go again sometime."

"I'll look forward to it," Snolan replied.

As she flapped her wings around to depart, Griffin said, "I am sorry about your family, Snolan."

Snolan smiled and exclaimed, "I have all the family I need." Then Griffin watched her disappear into the darkness.

THE BOW MAKER

The next day, Griffin was led by Sable into a small room of the castle. It was skimpy and square with a diamond–shaped window; this allowed the right amount of light to peer in. Looking toward the stone flooring, Griffin could see bundles upon bundles of wood. This wood Griffin did not recognize, for it had a red tint to it. To the right of the woodpiles sat a great amount of white stringing and a crate of small, arrow–shaped rocks. "This will be your weapon–making space. Meals will be brought to you regularly as you work," Sable explained.

"Sable, how many bows and arrow will you be needing exactly?" Griffin asked while wondering how much work he was getting himself into.

Sable started, "Let's just see how many you can come up with in the next day or two. Sound reasonable?"

"Yeah, sounds good, but, Sable, I don't have any tools for making these," Griffin responded.

"I think I have something in mind that would suit you," Sable said to him then exited the room. In moments he returned to Griffin holding a leather handbag. "Hope this will do. These were hers."

"Adria's?"

"Yes, Adria's."

Taking the bag from Sable, Griffin flipped it open carefully. The sack held a medium–sized hatchet with a blade that didn't look too friendly. He also found a small saw and a flashy pocket knife. Many other tools were found in the carrier. Each tool lay securely strapped in separate compartments of the bag. These devices were unmistakably well taken care of, and Griffin's eyes lit up at the sight of them.

"This is more than I got to work with back home!" Griffin eagerly said.

"So it will work then?" Sable anxiously asked.

"Yes! I'll have these done in no time," Griffin announced while admiring the hatchet.

"Great! Well, I will leave you to your work."

The boy first started with the long pieces of unfamiliar wood. Griffin used the hatchet with ease. He swiftly sliced the first piece of wood to be two feet in length. Picking up the unusual wood, he began to examine it. Griffin's mouth dropped open as he slowly bent the wood from left to right. It was like nothing he had ever worked with, and the wood flexed with incredible ease.

Setting the piece to the ground, he continued cutting from the blocks of wood. Although he made the pieces thin, the wood was still trustworthy. Griffin was precise in his work, and he made sure not one piece of lumber was larger or smaller than the other.

Two hours passed, and Griffin had completed chopping the wood that would soon be bows. It was evening, and no lunch had come to him. Griffin worked through his hunger and began the process of cutting the string. He cut each rope perfectly in length to fit a bow.

Fingertips aching and his stomach roaring, Griffin decided to finish for the day. He ran his hand through his messy hair and took in a deep gulp of air. The boy sighed. "That's enough for one day... I'll pick it back up tomorrow."

"Ah, Griffin." Sable poked his head in first then let the rest of his body inside the room. "I apologize that lunch did not make its way to you. I saw how intently you were working, and I did not wish to disturb you. Mogol will be in with some food for you shortly."

Sable left, and Griffin felt weary. In an instant, the boy was hit with an indescribable sensation. He felt consumed and alone. This was followed by an eerie voice in his head chanting, *Leave!* His brown eyes filled with confusion, and he grasped his aching head.

The voice seemed to die down, and the boy came to the conclusion that his hunger must be driving him mad. "Here you are, boy!" Mogol came treading toward Griffin with a plate covered in cooked fish meat. "You seemed to be making quite some progress," Mogol speculated, gazing at the piles of chopped wood. The boy ignored him and began to gobble the meal down. Mogol departed, and the strange voice seemed to leave when Griffin's appetite did.

The boy then made his way through the castle to the room where he was staying. He settled himself down on his bed for a quick rest, but that soon turned into a deep sleep.

There was Griffin at the Oval, standing before the whole Critin race. Dangling around his neck was the red diamond. All Critins were praising him for his accomplishments on bettering the Critin race. The satisfaction in himself overwhelmed every inch in his body. He felt loved. Griffin modestly smiled as each Critin thanked him immensely. And then with no forewarning there stood John. The boy ran toward him in sheer excitement. "John! John!

You wouldn't believe what has happened to me!" Griffin reached out to John. Before he got to him, John disappeared, and Griffin was now alone. A chilling voice pursued Griffin's mind. It demanded, "Leave them now, Griffin Dominic."

Skin soaked, heart pounding, and fear striking his senses, Griffin was awakened. With the words *Leave them now, Griffin Dominic* occupying his thoughts, he thankfully exclaimed, "It was just a dream, just a stupid dream."

Now having no desire for sleep, he placed his hands behind his head and began to think. Seeing John in his dream made him realize how much he already missed him. Thoughts of never seeing John again worried him.

An enormous strike hit the window, and Griffin was concerned it would break. "Snolan?" he hastily whispered while getting off the bed.

"Yes! It's me. How about another night flight? I thought I might give you a look at *their* side tonight."

Sleeping was out of the question at this point, and he replied while opening the window, "Well…all right, but who are *they?*"

"*They* are the Shriekian. Now take hold of your weapon and climb on," the hovering dragon commanded.

THE RETURN

As they soared, Griffin watched the moonlight touch the back of Snolan's scales. They sparkled intensely, and it reminded the boy of gems glistening in a pool of water. The moon was beautiful, and its radiance shone throughout the land. Adjusting the quiver on his back and his shortbow slung around his shoulder, Griffin said, "Why did you have me bring my bow? We aren't going to be running into any trouble tonight... are we?"

Snolan pushed a great load of air back with her wings and explained, "No, I do not expect you will need your weapon, but when being on Shriekian soil, it is best to have some source of protection."

After flying over the treetops several miles, Griffin grew anxious. He had wondered what the Shriekian would look like and act like, but he had never had the chance to ask. Also, part of him wanted to find out for himself.

The treetops below seemed to be never ending until there was an immense circle where no forest came into view. It looked like a patch missing out of a head of hair. In the middle of the treeless ring sat a gray and unhealthy–looking lake. "What is *that?*" Griffin asked in disgust.

Flying down toward the bog, Snolan replied, "That would be the Shriekian domain."

Griffin laughed. "The mighty Shriekian live in a swamp? You're joking. And the Critins who can fly *and* walk on land cannot defeat them?

"You see, Griffin: yes, the Critins can fly, and yes, the Shriekian live in water, but each are also land creatures. The Critins rule the sky, and the Shriekian rule the water, but they were both given land to share. The Shriekian want the land to themselves, and they are determined to succeed. They almost succeeded when the—"

"Slaughter," Griffin intervened. "I heard Sable's father saved the Critin race."

"Yes, he was a brave leader," Snolan said as they landed on the edge of the marshy lake.

Griffin stepped off the dragon, and immediately his sneakers began to sink into the brown muck. Snolan's four legs were already consumed in the thick sludge. They pulled their feet out with much effort and trailed backward in hopes of reaching solid ground. Finding his footing, Griffin kicked off some loose mud and asked sarcastically, "So how do these beings walk on land? Do they just hop out of the water and sprout legs?"

"So you have heard a little about the Shriekian?" Snolan said.

"What?" the boy questioned. "I was joking. That doesn't really happen … does it?"

"You would be surprised." She smiled.

As they ventured around the outer edges of the lake, the stench became almost unbearable. The water was unbelievably thick and rich with bacteria and appeared green. Bubbles rose to the surface, and, when popping, they let out a green smog that dissolved in the air. Griffin wondered, "How do we know the Shriekian aren't coming now? Couldn't they just pop out of the water and attack us?" The boy's eyes were fixed on a bubble rising to the surface of the lake.

"You would have knowledge of them coming before you even saw them. Trust me," Snolan said with certainty.

"But how do you…" But then Griffin stopped, for something caught his eye across the lake. "Snolan, what's that?" he said while pointing his finger at something large and glistening in the moonlight on the other side of the water.

"Oh that!" Snolan exclaimed. "That's an old prison they used to keep their people in if they did not obey. It would be smart not to go near it."

"Well, I want to go look at it. Come on. You said it yourself: if we were in danger, we would know it." Griffin began running around the edge of the lake toward the gray prison. His feet again sank down in the sludge, and mud flew into the air as he ran. Snolan trailed behind him, trying to dodge the flying dirt particles that Griffin was kicking up. The lake was large, and, catching his breath, Griffin finally reached his destination. Dropping to his knees, he grabbed the top of his head and exclaimed, "Oh my God."

Walking up behind Griffin was Snolan. Before looking in the pen, she exclaimed, "What was so important that you had to run halfway across Aranwea to…" But then Snolan stopped, for when she looked to see what had Griffin so distraught, she too could not believe her eyes.

It was her, Adria Heprum. There she lay in a large, barred jail that rose high into the air. She looked like a caged animal in a zoo that had not been tended to in weeks. Her prison was about ten feet wide, and inside it held a small crate used for shelter from the rain. Her eyes were closed, and her head rested motionless next to a stagnant bowl of water and a stale bit of food. Her long, brown hair was tangled and unclean. The heels of her feet had sores. "No, no… no! It cannot be! They took her! She was killed more than a year ago!" Snolan exclaimed, thrusting her mighty head from left to right.

"Well, obviously not! And you an–and the Critins just abandoned her!" Griffin shouted in rage.

"Sable announced her dead, Griffin, so we all thought—"

"Sable? Sable is a weak leader!" Griffin interrupted while gripping the cage bars with all his might. "We are not leaving without her."

Griffin became mesmerized in finding a solution that would release Adria. He frantically searched the prison as if nothing else in the world mattered. "What are you looking for?" the dragon questioned. She was peering around as if she were keeping lookout for a predator.

"Some sort of lock," he replied.

"A lock? What's that?"

"It's a metal piece used to keep things trapped inside…" Griffin stopped. He had found the lock he was looking for, but the location of it was much too high for him to reach. Worried and frustrated, the boy gripped his head.

Setting his bow and quiver on the ground, he exclaimed, "Snolan! You see that shiny silver thing dangling up there?"

"Yes." Snolan was gazing up at the metal lock.

"We break that, and Adria is free," he said, pointing the metal piece out.

"Let me see what I can do," Snolan announced.

Getting on her hind legs, Snolan attempted to bite the rusted lock. She slowly elongated her neck to full length, but the lock was still out of the reach of her mouth. Gradually, Snolan drew her face away from the metal lock and puffed her cheeks. Jolting her face forward, she set free a mouthful of blazing flames. The metal piece seemed to stand untouched. The only effect the fire had was turning the lock a shade darker.

Realizing the attempt to burn the lock was a failure, Snolan pushed her front legs off the prison and returned to her all fours. Griffin closed his eyes and shook his head in despair. "We will find a way, Griffin," the dragon said with certainty. "Even if we have to go back and get help, we will find a way."

Opening his eyes, he stated, "There is *no* time to get help. Adria needs us now! That is if we are not already too late."

"Well..." Snolan glanced around for an answer when her eyes landed on Griffin's shortbow. "Hey, Griffin! How about your bow thing?"

His eyes widened with hopefulness. Griffin rushed over to his bow and quiver. He took an arrow and his shortbow and positioned himself a few feet away from the lock. He set up the weapon so it was ready to discharge the arrow. Griffin then aimed it directly at the silver piece that kept him from getting to Adria. One eye shut, he noticed the words *Steady Eye and Fire.* The boy's aim was flawless. Pulling back on the string, he released his hand from the feathered tail of the arrow.

The lock was hit! Not only was it hit, but the arrow was driven straight through the key-hole, causing the arrow and the lock to break into many pieces. The barred door the lock had held up crashed to the ground before Griffin and Snolan's feet. "Yes!" Griffin leapt in excitement.

"You did it!" Snolan exclaimed.

Tossing his weapon to the forest floor, Griffin ran over to the entrance of the cage. He stepped inside cautiously. "Adria," he whispered.

She gave no response. Again he tried. "Adria, can you hear me? I'm going to get you out of here." Again she sent back no response, and Griffin feared her time had ended.

Snolan stuck her face in the prison directly above Adria. Nudging her with her nose, the dragon started, "Adria, wake up. It's Snolan."

Suddenly Adria's eyes began to flicker. She fully opened them and turned her head to face Griffin and the dragon. She muttered with much effort, "S–S–Snolan?" Then her head fell back, and her body once again went limp and motionless.

"We need to get her back to the castle now!" Snolan demanded. But Griffin just sat on his knees unable to move, for when Adria turned her face he knew exactly who she was. "Griffin!

Griffin! Come on, you can obviously see she is not well!" the dragon desperately bellowed.

Setting his last thought aside, Griffin replied, "Yes, yes, let's get her out of here."

In an instant, the earth began to move and rumble. The ground seemed to shake like an uneasy sea, and more and more bubbles began to rise from the smoggy lake. Griffin stood up and struggled to stay upright. Hands stretched outward to help keep his balance, Griffin yelled, "Snolan! What's going on?"

Looking toward the lake Snolan announced, "It's them! Grab her, and get on and with haste!"

Griffin drew up Adria in his arms. She was lifeless. The intensity of the quake was so powerful he could barely carry her out of the cage. The dragon kneeled down and said in a panic, "Hurry! Put her on my back!" Griffin hurriedly but carefully placed the unresponsive girl on Snolan's scale–covered back, snatched his bow and quiver, and then got on himself. Branches and roots snapped all around them as the trembling became more powerful. The dragon worked her wings with all their might, and they began to take flight. "Now brace yourself!" she demanded. Snolan extended her wingspan to full length, and with a sudden swipe of her wings, they were beyond the forest trees. Griffin, supporting both himself and Adria on Snolan looked back at what they had just escaped. Elevating out of the depths' marshy abyss was something so large it consumed half the lake. "Snolan! Did you see what was rising out of the Shriekian Lake?" Griffin shouted in disbelief.

"Yes..." Then she paused. "The Shriekian domain."

The Shriekian domain was a black, forbidding castle. It looked nothing like the Critins' home, for it had an eerie sense about it. The Shriekians' black walls rose high into the air, and the front of the fortress owned a drawbridge. As it finished rising, water flushed out of it like a washcloth being rung dry. "Th–the Shriekian domain? But won't they notice that Adria broke free?" Griffin stuttered, looking at the motionless body that lay in his lap.

Snolan flapped her wings a bit harder in the direction of the Critin castle and replied, "For the sake of the Critin race and ourselves...I pray not."

GRIFFIN'S ANGER

Snolan landed on the ground in front of the castle. Griffin carefully took Adria in his arms once again and began to carry her inside the castle's entrance. The doors started to open before Griffin got to them. Stepping outside was Sable. "Where have you..." Sable's words then stopped. Sable made eye contact with Griffin and back to Adria then back to Griffin. He gasped. "No, no, no! It is impossible! The Shriekian took her! Just as they took Vector!"

Glaring into Sable's eyes, the maddened boy bellowed, "You sicken me! You are a disgrace to call yourself a leader!"

Sable, looking as if he had just witnessed an apparition, stuttered, "I thought they must have … I thought they had to have killed her." Sable then reached out to touch the lifeless face of Adria.

Griffin moved so Adria was out of his reach and replied with loathing, "That's the thing. You *thought* they had killed her. But did you *ever* go look for her? Did you *ever* think that she still might be alive only living with them … suffering!" Griffin gazed at Adria with worry. "God knows what she went through. You may just need to find a new way to win your war." Griffin brushed past Sable and nudged the half–opened doors with his shoulder.

Sable stood in a state of shock. Snolan, witnessing the conversation, spoke. "Sable, you didn't know." The confused, feathered being felt so completely disgusted with himself. Sable then took flight and disappeared into the moonlight.

Back in Griffin's room, he set Adria down on his bed. He situated the brown and green blankets across her body and knelt down next to her. "This should have never happened.

You're going to be all right." Griffin then left the room.

He returned moments later holding a large glass of water, and once again the boy knelt down to the bedside. "Adria, can you hear me?" he whispered to the stationary body. "You are safe now. Wake up." He nudged her cold arm with his hand.

Again her eyes began to rapidly open and close until she found the strength to fully open them. Gaining consciousness, she abruptly sat up and shouted, "I–I'm sorry! I'll go back to the cage! Just please don't hurt me!"

"Adria, you are back with the Critins!" Griffin explained, quickly standing up. Lungs breathing heavily, she mumbled, "A human? But how? How did I get here?"

"My name is Griffin. Snolan and I rescued you from the Shriekian. You are not well. Here's some water," Griffin said, offering her the glass.

"No, no! I shouldn't be here!" She was frantically shaking her head. Adria tried to lift the rest of her body out of the bed, but a wave of dizziness hit her, and her head fell back to the pillow.

"Adria! You are not well! You cannot tell me that you want to leave and go back to *them!*" Griffin exclaimed.

Struggling to breathe, she stammered, "I never want to go back to them, b–but I cannot stay here."

"Please … please just drink this," he begged. Adria sat up once more, and Griffin handed her the glass of water. She drank it as though water hadn't touched her mouth in ages.

"I must go," she said when the last drop of water was gone. She tossed him the empty cup and stepped off the bed with wobbly legs.

Griffin knew she could not leave, for Adria surely would not make it. Griffin started, "Everyone thought you were dead."

She stopped before reaching the door. "When anyone is taken by them … they are assumed dead. It's the way it is."

"Yeah … well, everyone back home thought you were dead too."

"You don't know anything about my home life," she snapped.

"You wouldn't believe the look on the class's face. Mrs. Showl came into the classroom wearing that stupid yellow hat that she always wore." Griffin laughed. "When she came through the doors to greet the class...I knew something was different."

Adria, now intrigued by the conversation, turned away from the door and sat on the bed. Griffin continued, "I knew something was different because her usual upbeat face was worried. I'm not exactly sure how she said it, but she told us how you went missing, and the whole class became very concerned. One girl wouldn't stop bawling for hours. What was her name? Blonde hair...pigtails...What was her name?

"Lisa Crawford." Adria gasped in disbelief. "She was my best friend."

"Yeah, that was it!" Griffin said.

Adria looked up at Griffin's face as if she were examining him. Adria narrowed her eyes and exclaimed, "Griffin Dominic? Wow...I...I can't believe it!" She thrust her arms around him. "It's so good to see a familiar face! Honestly, it's so good to see another human."

"So you do remember me?" Griffin laughed, his cheeks reddening.

Adria freed Griffin and said, "Of course. Who could forget the boy that spent more time in the principal's office than the actual classroom?" Griffin regretted that she remembered that about him.

Griffin noticed Adria's eyes were becoming heavy, and she struggled to keep them open. Still standing before her, Griffin pleaded, "Adria, please rest. Just for tonight rest here."

She thought to herself a bit and said, "Well, maybe just for tonight. But in the morning, I'll be leaving right away." Adria then lowered her body on the bed and went to sleep within seconds.

The boy positioned himself on the stone floor with his hand resting behind his head. He got into a deep thought of what had just happened in the past couple of hours. *She's safe. I saved Adria Heprum,* he thought. Then Griffin dozed off into slumber, feeling quite happy with himself.

Griffin was woken up the next morning to the squeaking of the door. He sat up, and, brushing the sleep away from his eyes, he saw Mogol standing in the doorway. He was carrying two plates of food, which made it hard for him to open the door. Peering at the sleeping Adria, Mogol said, "Thought you guys could use something to satisfy your hunger." Griffin said nothing but instead he stared off into the opposite direction of Mogol. "Well, I'll just leave this here." Mogol placed the steaming fish on the wooden table and exited the room.

The aroma of the freshly cooked meat found Griffin's nose, and his stomach ached with hunger. Images of the moldy food that lay next to Adria in her prison passed through his mind, and he realized Adria's body must be starved.

Griffin got to his feet with much effort, for his back was sore from sleeping on the firm surface. The boy grabbed a plate and went to wake her. She looked so peaceful and deep in slumber that Griffin was unsure if he should wake her. He stood debating whether to call her name or not when she opened her eyes and gasped, "What are you doing?"

Startled and a little embarrassed, the boy stepped backward and replied, "I–I'm sorry, I was just coming to wake you. You must be hungry." Griffin pushed the plate toward her.

Sitting up, she brushed her hair out of hair eyes and took the food. Griffin took a seat at the table, and Adria immediately started to eat the fish as if it were her last meal. Griffin started consuming his meal also. Adria, with a mouthful of food, asked, "So... how'd you get involved with the Critins?"

Excited that she was willing to consider a conversation, Griffin explained, "Well, I just kinda came across them I guess.

"I'm surprised they took in another human after what I did to their kind," Adria said with much shame.

"But it wasn't your fault," Griffin quickly replied. "They had control of you. Don't the Critins realize that?"

"How do you know this?" she asked.

Griffin walked over to the bedside and reached underneath it. He pulled out the journal. "This." Griffin showed her.

"My journal!" she said. Adria took it from him and eagerly flipped through the pages. "Sable gave this to me on my birthday." Suddenly she looked very displeased. "So you thought you could just go through my journal?"

"What? Well...I looked through it, and there wasn't much writing. Plus, I thought you were—"

"Dead?" Adria interrupted.

"Well, yeah," Griffin said uneasily.

Setting the journal aside, she then asked, "So why are you here anyways?"

"Sable thinks I can help them," Griffin explained. "When I first ran into Sable and Mogol in the woods, it was very obvious how they felt about humans. They were going to kill me."

"So how'd you get out of it?"

"With this." Griffin took his shortbow from the corner. "They want me to train their army to fight with a bow and arrow. Sable thinks with this unfamiliar weapon they can beat the Shriekian."

Confused, Adria exclaimed in disbelief, "Wait, what? Sable wants to go to war? Are you sure?"

"Well, yeah, that's what he told the villagers last night. But I don't think I'm staying. I can't live here knowing they abandoned you," Griffin replied.

"I went to them!" she shouted. "The Critins don't understand what power the Shriekian have over humans. This is no cowardly race if that's what you are thinking, and Sable is a great leader. You need to stay and help them win their freedom." Her dark brown eyes were piercing Griffin's every emotion.

"No, no, are you crazy?" The boy stuttered. "I sure am not ending up in a metal crate on the verge of death like you, Adria. They are cowards for not coming and finding you!"

"Sable did what was necessary for his kind!" She stood up to face him. "You are the coward."

Standing face to face with Adria, Griffin commanded, "I guess saving you was a mistake. Sorry, won't happen again. I'm leaving, and I suggest you do the same."

Appearing in the doorway again, Mogol exclaimed, "Don't mean to interrupt, but Sable wants to see you both at the Oval. He is waiting."

Turning back to Adria, Griffin announced, "Perfect...I'll tell him that I'm leaving now."

The two of them left the room and made their way up the staircase to the Oval. Not a word was spoken between them until they reached the entrance to where Sable waited. Griffin stopped before entering, which caused Adria to stop also. "Look, I'm glad we could get you away from the Shriekian. Don't get me wrong. But the villagers don't want me here any more than they want you here."

"If you saved their race, I'm sure they wouldn't mind you staying," Adria said. She then pushed past him and opened the door to the Oval. Griffin trailed behind her.

Sable stood looking out into the vast land with his back facing Adria and Griffin. Hearing them approach, he turned around. "Adria, words cannot express my emotions. You are alive and well. I have a sickened feeling in my stomach when I think of what you went through. I cannot apologize enough. I thought you were forever gone." Sable looked to the ground in shame.

"You don't need to apologize, Sable. I know you couldn't do anything for me. I should be apologizing, not you. I told the Shriekian of your weakness," Adria said in sorrow.

"You had no control over that; this I know. I am just filled with happiness to see you again." Sable smiled.

Sable tried to explain to them that if they stayed he would see to it that the villagers accepted them. This he promised. Griffin said nothing and focused his eyes on anything but Sable. Adria, on the other hand, was paying close attention to every word that Sable was saying. She took in every word that left Sable's mouth, and her eyes gleamed with happiness as Sable spoke to them. "Griffin," he exclaimed. Griffin's wandering eyes were directed toward Sable. "We cannot win this war without you."

"Adria and I are leaving Aranwea," Griffin replied.

"I'm staying," she said.

Griffin's eyes widened. "You–you're what?"

"I brought this doom to your kind, Sable. It wouldn't be right for me to leave," she declared, glancing at Griffin.

Frustrated, Griffin ruffled his shaggy hair. "You can't be serious? You're staying after they left you to die?"

"Yes, I'm staying," she replied. Griffin stormed out of the Oval without saying another word.

THE FIRST OF MANY

Adria found Griffin back in his room. She started, "You are not a coward. I'm sorry for what I said earlier." Ignoring her, Griffin continued to gather his possessions. "You were brave to save me. The Critins need you, as I needed you at the lake." Adria walked over to him and grabbed his arm. "Please, Griffin... stay."

Griffin stared into her dark brown eyes and sighed, "I can't. They aren't loyal beings. If they were, they would not have left you." Griffin pulled away from her grip and finished collecting his belongings. He started for the door but then stopped. "What is that?" Griffin asked in confusion.

"What's what? I didn't say anything. But Griffin, please don't go. Just let me explain…"

"No, no, not you!" he bellowed. "The voices." Griffin became overwhelmed with a commanding voice striking fear and desire into his thoughts. It was a snaky tone that spoke to him, speaking many things at the same time. Griffin dropped his bows and quiver and fell to his knees in agony. He clutched his consumed head with his hands. *Leave them! Come find us, Griffin Dominic!* The controlling voice, which only Griffin could hear, beckoned his every desire. Adria ran over and knelt down to his side. Griffin was sweating uncontrollably as he sat hunched over. The boy hollered, "Leave me alone! Leave me alone!"

"Griffin! Griffin! It's them! It's the Shriekian! Look at me! Focus on my eyes!" she shouted in a panic. The voice became louder, and it seemed as if a radio was set to full force in his ears. Eyes now bloodshot, he could only see Adria's words being mouthed to him.

Then the voices stopped all at once. Breathing heavily, Griffin turned over to lie on his back. Adria's face was filled with concern. "It was them, Griffin," she said softly.

Wiping some sweat away from his forehead, Griffin muttered, "What do they want from me?" Griffin could barely speak, for his whole body trembled.

"They must know you are a great threat to them."

"Is this what happened to you?"

"Yes."

"Does it get worse?"

"Yes."

"But why?" Griffin's hands were still shaking a bit. "What do they want with humans?"

Getting up off the floor, she said, "I'll tell you what I know, but sit down. I know what it feels like to be attacked by them."

Adria helped him get up off the ground, and they both sat on the wooden bed. Adria pushed the blankets to the side. "After I came to Aranwea, I felt loved. For once in my life, I felt like I truly was where I was meant to be. Mogol and Sable found me one morning not far from my house. I had run away and soon found myself lost in the forest. They took me to their home and treated me like just another Critin. They treated me like we had no differences. A year and a half later, I never wanted to leave until…" Adria paused. "They started to get to me, the Shriekian I mean. They soon began to attack almost daily. Each time they attacked, it was harder for me to resist. One day, it was too much, and I–I went to them. I was hypnotized—mesmerized by the power they had over me. I would not tell them the Critins' weakness until I couldn't take the torture anymore and it was too much for me to handle. Once I had told them what they wanted to know…I thought they would let me go. But they kept me because they wanted more than to know the Critins' weakness."

"What more could they want from you?"

"One night when I was being held in the Shriekians' castle, I overheard two of the creatures talking. They spoke of humans and how we could become a greater power than them. They said if I was able to resist their last effort to bring me to their side, I would have been given unique gifts," Adria explained.

"Unique gifts? What kind of gifts?"

"I do not know, Griffin. All I know is they are either scared of this human power or they think they can somehow use it."

He shook his head. "But you couldn't resist them … right?"

"No."

"Then you lost this power that you maybe could have gotten right? So why would they still keep you alive? Why wouldn't they just kill you?"

"I think they just kept me in hopes that it would come back to me. But it's gone. I know it is."

"Maybe it will come back!" Griffin exclaimed.

Shaking her head, she replied, "No, it won't, and I can't say I would want these powers either."

Placing his hand on her shoulder, Griffin said, "Well, I'm sorry all this happened to you, and I'm glad you are safe now, but I obviously don't belong here. All this...it's over my head. I'm really sorry, but you can leave with me if you like." Griffin sat waiting for her reply.

"Griffin...there is a reason why you left your home. A sixteen–year–old boy wouldn't just leave his perfect home life without a reason."

"My home life has nothing to do with—"

"That's the thing. You don't have a perfect home life, and you left with the Critins for the same reason I left with them," she interrupted.

"And what reason might that be?" Griffin questioned, crossing his arms.

"To find something better."

Griffin was motionless. Deep inside of him, he knew she was right, whether he wanted to acknowledge it or not.

"You know you must stay and win this war," she ended softly. Adria's eyes were gleaming and focused on Griffin's. She waited for his next words as if the world's greatest secret were about to be told.

Every emotion of dislike toward the Critins melted away from Griffin's mind. "I will stay with you a–and the Critins." Griffin smiled gently.

She threw her arms around Griffin and cried, "I knew it! I knew you would! Thank you, Griffin, thank you! You will win this war!"

She let go of him. "We will win this war together," he ended.

THEIR STORIES

Once they found Sable, they told him the news that Griffin would be staying. He was awestruck, for he thought it was for certain that Griffin had his mind set to leave. "Thank you, Griffin. You will forever be remembered in Aranwea," Sable proudly said to him.

Griffin said, "And I am sorry for what I said last night. It wasn't right for me to say those things."

Nodding his head, Sable exclaimed, "There is no need for apologies. Now, we have much to talk about. Griffin, how fast can you finish making those weapons?"

"It shouldn't take longer than a day or two."

"And I'll help him," Adria added.

"That should be about right. By the next week…we shall be ready for battle," Sable announced.

Adria, Sable, and Griffin made their way back down the spiral staircase of the castle. When they reached the bottom, Sable turned to Adria. "You must be longing for a better wardrobe, Adria. Seek out Methia; I'm sure you haven't forgotten where to find her." Sable smiled.

"I haven't forgotten anything about this place," she replied then looked to Griffin. "I'll be right in to help with the weapon making when I'm finished."

Griffin nodded his head, and she left down one of the hallways. "Griffin," Sable started, "do make sure Adria doesn't strain herself. She has been through more than we can imagine, and I wish her to rest."

"Okay, Sable," Griffin agreed. Then he went to the room to continue his bow making. He had already finished cutting the wood to make the bows the day prior and sliced the strings to fit it. So he first started to string the bows and decided the arrow–making process could wait. The boy worked quickly but still maintained quality in his weapon making. Griffin placed one end of the newly cut wood at the top of his foot and flexed the other end of the bow down with his hand. Once again, Griffin was astounded with how well the stick curved to make the perfect shape of a bow. Grabbing a string, the boy tightly wrapped it around each end of the bow. When he had finished tying the string, the bow was complete. "One down," Griffin said out loud.

A few hours later, Griffin had a total of thirty bows made when Adria stepped in the room. What she was wearing looked nothing like the clothing he was accustomed to. Adria appeared to be dressed in brown leather garments, which flowed with black feathers from the sides. Her dark brown hair reached past her shoulders and was no longer tattered or tangled. Adria's eyes didn't have near the amount of tiredness lingering about them anymore but instead shone bright and full of life. She seemed to be a completely different person than when Griffin had found her.

Griffin gawked at her.

"So you like the Critins' clothing?" Adria grabbed the bottom of her long–sleeved shirt. "I'm sure you'll be getting a set soon."

Griffin said nothing at first, then stammered, "Oh … oh yeah, I think Sable said something about that the first day I was here."

Griffin watched her as she sat down on the floor next to him. Picking up one of the smaller pieces of wood, Griffin asked, "So do you know what this type of wood is?" He gave it to Adria.

Adria took the stick that would soon be made into a bow. She studied it for an instant, bending it sideways with ease. Gazing up at him, she handed it back and replied, "This is a Stignatoria branch. It's a very rare branch that only grows on the limbs of a Stignatoria tree. Why would you need this for making bows?"

"Well … I told Sable I would be needing bendable wood to do the job. But with this flexible wood it should take a lot less time,"

Griffin responded then started with his work once again.

Adria looked about the small square room that Griffin was working in. Her eyes landed on the bag of tools that once belonged to her. "My tool bag! I brought that from home!" Adria exclaimed.

Griffin stopped his work once more and looked at the leather bag. "Sable gave it to me to make these bows. I'm not too far from being done, so you can have them back."

"Oh no, I don't need them. I'm glad they could help you. So how can I help?"

"Don't worry about it, Adria. You have been through a lot, and it shouldn't take much longer. You just rest." Griffin offered.

"I'll know when I need to rest. I'm fine. I want to help."

Having no desire to begin a fight with her, Griffin assigned Adria the simple task of slicing the remaining wood into small pieces the size of arrows.

They worked in silence with only the sounds of their hands busy at work cutting, bending and slicing the thick tree into handmade artillery. Griffin started, "Adria, why did you leave home? I mean I know you weren't happy there, but why?"

Adria was working very swiftly and in no time had a stack of thin wood ready to be finished into arrows. Adria sighed. "Well…Dad was more interested in drugs than my mom and me. My mom couldn't take it anymore, and she left. She said she would be back for me, but she never came back. I don't really blame her. I wouldn't go back to him either. Well…one night it was just too much, and I ran away. You know the rest. So what about you? What's your story?"

Griffin bent one of the bows into place and quickly tied the strings off on each end. He set it on top of the pile of the finished bows. "Well, my dad never wanted kids to begin with. He told me that many times. So, when they had me, it seemed like no matter how hard I tried I just wasn't good enough for him. I eventually just stopped trying, and my mom got bored of having me around."

"That's horrible. I can't imagine not wanting your own kid."

"Don't feel sorry for me!" Griffin exclaimed. "You had a worse home life; then you got stuck with the Shriekian. I can't believe what you have gone through."

Looking to the ground Adria paused. She started to cut the wood once again and said, "I don't know, Griffin. I'm just glad that's over with now." She smiled toward him.

Finishing another weapon, Griffin asked, "Adria, if you don't mind me asking, what *did* the Shriekian put you through exactly?"

Adria flipped her hair out of her eyes and replied, "I'd rather not talk about this. Maybe someday but just not now."

"I–I'm sorry; I should have known," Griffin uneasily responded.

They continued to work for the next few hours. The two of them found the labor went by much faster in each other's company. Adria and Griffin were much alike in some aspects, and they found that to be true as they conversed.

Griffin settled down to see how much they had accomplished. He was shocked at what they had completed as he gazed at the fifty–five bows and the eight stacks of thin wood that would be turned into arrows. "I think that's enough for a day. We should be done by tomorrow." Griffin sighed.

Setting the last sliver of wood on one of the mounds, Adria exclaimed, "Good, because I'm starved."

Adria and Griffin left the weapon–making room and went to search for Mogol. Being late in the afternoon, hunger had overtaken them, and they had worked many hours without rest. The two of them eventually located Mogol, and he then fed them until their stomachs were filled. After dinner Griffin and Adria said good night and went to find sleep in their separate rooms of the castle.

Griffin, though undoubtedly tired, did not go to sleep. As soon as he and Adria parted, the boy went straight back to the weapons room and continued working through the night until his fingers throbbed with soreness. Having the arrow wood already cut made the process go by faster, but he still had much to do. The boy wound the pointed rock pieces tightly at the end of each of the thinned wood and cut a small slit in the other end, which the bow's string would lie between. Using tree sap, Griffin pasted Critin feathers on the end of the arrows for stability and balance. Griffin worked by candlelight throughout the night until his eyes grew heavy with tiredness and he slumped over and went to sleep.

"Griffin, Griffin, wake up," Adria whispered.

Flashing his eyes open then closed for a moment, the boy sat up. It was morning. Looking around, Griffin realized he hadn't made it back to his room the night before. Feeling the discomfort in his lower back from sleeping on hard arrows, he said, "I guess I wasn't as tired as I thought last night."

Adria crossed her arms and spouted, "I would have helped you finish these! You said we were done for the day."

Griffin slowly got to his feet, still holding his aching back. Shaking the tiredness off, Griffin responded, "Adria, Sable told me to let you rest. I knew if I kept working you would too."

Looking rather displeased, she replied, "Well, I was fine. How much did you get done?"

Gazing around at the numerous scattered and completed arrows, Griffin said, "Well, it looks like we are about done."

Popping in the doorway was Sable. "Were you two working all through the night?" Stepping inside he was careful not to tread on any of the handmade weapons.

"No," Adria said. "I didn't, but Griffin did."

Looking to Griffin, Sable asked hopefully, "So are you about finished then?"

Checking the premises once more, the boy replied, "I probably will need to make a few more arrows. It won't take long, but I can start training your soldiers at any time."

"Great, Griffin! You will begin training after the hour of noon." Sable smiled at Griffin then exited the room.

Adria started, "I could have helped you last night; you don't have to try to be the hero by yourself."

Throwing his hands in the air, Griffin laughed, and his cheeks reddened. "I'm not trying to be!"

TRAINING BEGINS

"Listen up!" Sable shouted to the fifty Critin soldiers that were all assembled in a horizontal line. Every one of the Critins had a leather bag filled with arrows slung across his body and a bow in his hand. "War is near, and we shall be prepared." Sable was pacing up and down the row of warriors. He pointed his talon at Griffin. "You will listen to this boy to the best of your abilities. You *all* shall do as he commands in the next few days, or you will surely regret it." Sable flashed his eyes toward Vetch. Vetch looked as though he was suffering to be present with a human. Sable walked to Griffin's side and stated, "I will leave you to your work. If anything should arise, come find me."

Sable flew off toward the castle, and Griffin was left with the Critin army. Their training ground was a large lush green field that was just to the side of the forest. With his shortbow in hand and quiver of arrows on his back, Griffin said, "Well, as you all know, I'm supposed to be teaching you how to use a bow."

"Yeah! Why else would we be here!" One of the soldiers smirked. The rest of the army chuckled in approval.

"Right," Griffin said. "Well, I'll show you a few examples on how to shoot a bow first." Griffin placed the arrow on the bow's string and released the arrow past the forest trees. Many of the Critins gasped in awe at what they had just witnessed. Vetch did not seem to care.

Pleased with the reaction he got from the majority of the soldiers, Griffin proceeded. "Now, first off, you will need to set the tail of the arrow on the bow's string." Showing them the end of the arrow, he added, "There is a small crevice at the end of each arrow, and you will need to place the string in it." The warriors appeared to be listening closely. "Once the arrow is in place, you pull the arrow and string back toward you." Griffin drew the string back with the arrow and held it in place. "Once you have it locked in position, you take aim and..." Before Griffin could finish his last words, his back was struck with a stone that caused him to unwillingly release the arrow into the air.

Griffin dropped his bow and quiver and turned toward Vetch with a loathing face.

"What are you going to do, boy?" Vetch stepped out of the line toward Griffin. "Are you going to run to Sable? Maybe cower behind him just like at the Oval?"

Griffin hurriedly stormed to Vetch, standing but a few feet from him. "I'd say you're the coward, Vetch. If you want to fight, don't throw pebbles." Vetch drew back his talon, and before Griffin could react, he thrust his claws across Griffin's face. Clutching his bloody cheek, Griffin lunged toward Vetch but was heaved back by someone tugging at his arm. Griffin drew his clenched fist back to hit the one who had prevented him from getting to his foe, but when he turned around, he let his fist down.

It was Adria, and she pleaded, "Griffin, stop! Stop, Griffin!"

Fighting to free himself of her grip, Griffin shouted, "Let go of me!"

"Griffin!" Adria screamed.

Then Griffin stopped, for he saw the distress on her face.

Vetch spoke, "So it is true? Adria Heprum is living with the Critins once again. How does it feel to have doomed us all?"

"You are a sick creature! Come on, Griffin." Adria yanked at his arm.

"Go on, boy. Go tell Sable you can't handle it here." Vetch's cat eyes were penetrating Griffin.

Moving his arm from Adria's hold, Griffin replied, "No."

"What?" Adria gasped. "You're going to get hurt. Now come on."

Griffin faced her. "I'll be fine. Bring me a rag." His face was dripping blood as he spoke. Shaking her head in disapproval, Adria left.

Griffin walked back to gather his bow and quiver and smiled. "So where were we?"

Vetch appeared to be exceedingly angry and made his way back in line. Adria returned to Griffin quickly with a dampened towel. The boy wiped his stinging face, showing no sign of pain, then continued to teach them the ways of the bow.

For the next hour, Griffin showed the army the basics of archery. They all took note of what Griffin was trying to show them, and he seemed to have gained some respect of the army. Even Vetch was learning fast, but never would he make eye contact with Griffin.

Griffin walked up and down the line of soldiers answering any question they had to offer. "I just can't get the arrow to go where I want it to," a frustrated Critin said to Griffin.

"Let me see you shoot it," Griffin replied. The creature stretched his arms away from his body and wings as he got ready to shoot it. The boy studied the Critin closely as he released the arrow. "Here's your problem." Pretending to shoot an arrow, Griffin moved his drawn elbow arm up and down. "You've got to keep your elbow up when you are letting go of the strings. Now, try again."

Taking in Griffin's words, the soldier did as he was told. Again, extending his arms outward, the Critin discharged the arrow with absolute control. Looking very pleased, the Critin lowered the bow and exclaimed, "Thanks…ummm…"

"Griffin," the boy said.

"Griffin! Thank you, Griffin. My name is Zocah."

"Well, if you have any more questions, Zocah, just let me know." Griffin smiled and made his way back down the line.

Adria sat in the grass a few yards away. She watched Griffin as he directed the Critin army. A couple hours later, they had finished for the day. Before they left, Griffin said to all, "You all are learning very fast. Tomorrow we will work more on aiming."

Wind brushed past his sore face as the Critins flew away. Griffin placed his hand on his cheek to keep the wind from brushing past it further. Adria stood up as Griffin walked back to the castle in her direction. "You don't need to watch over me, you know. I was fine back there," Griffin said as they made their way out of the field.

"You looked like you could have used some help to me. Griffin, don't pick fights with the Critins. You don't know what they are capable of."

"If you were watching, I wasn't starting anything. I'm just going to have to deal with him," the boy responded, touching his throbbing face.

Adria quickly moved his hand away. "Don't touch it! It's going to get infected. I have some stuff back at the castle that will help it."

Standing at the basin of the castle was Snolan, and she flew them to the entrance. Adria and Griffin entered the castle, and Sable immediately stopped them, "So how did it…" Sable ended his words when he saw Griffin's face. "Griffin, *what* happened? I told you to come seek me out if they gave you trouble."

"Sable, it's okay. We got off to a bad start, but we got a lot done today. They are learning very fast."

"That is good to hear," Sable answered. "Adria, will you tend to Griffin's wound?" Adria nodded her head and once again took Griffin by the arm.

"Adria, I'm fine!" Griffin protested as he was nearly being dragged down the hallway by Adria. "It's just a scratch; it'll heal just fine."

Adria took him to a tiny room in the castle. She set him down on a wooden stool and examined his face thoroughly. Griffin sat impatiently as she looked him over. "Well, you would probably be getting stitches, but being here, we don't have that option."

She took a wet rag and carefully cleaned the individual scrapes. Griffin drew his face back in pain as she touched the exposed flesh. Adria then took a bowl of what looked to be different color leaves and began to grind them with a round wooden piece. Adria sprinkled a bit of water on the crushed leaves and mixed it together. She scooped some of the dampened leaves in her hand and said to him, "This may hurt a little, but it will stop infection better than anything you can find back home."

She smeared it directly on Griffin's lacerations. Griffin clenched his teeth and pulled away from her when she was through putting it on. "It may hurt a little?" Griffin exclaimed as he threatened to touch his throbbing cheek. "This hurts more than when it actually happened!"

"It will stop soon; just don't touch it," Adria reassured as she put the bowl away. "You really love it, don't you?"

Still wincing with pain, Griffin asked, "Love what? The feeling of my face on fire? Oh yeah, feels great."

Adria's tossed her face. "No, no, I mean you really love teaching them. I can tell."

"It's all right. I mean I don't hate it. I'm just trying to help Sable out."

Adria walked toward the door and stopped. "I think you like it more than you know." Before she left she added, "Leave the herb on your face for a few more minutes, then take the towel and clean it off. Good night."

"Good night," Griffin replied as he watched her leave the room.

During the next couple days, Griffin devoted most of his time to training Sable's army. Adria was indeed correct. As the days passed, he realized how much he adored teaching this skill. Griffin not only had a passionate approach toward archery but also had a love for passing on his knowledge of it. Not a question from a warrior about a bow and arrow went unanswered. The boy worked them exceptionally hard, making sure their archery skills reached their full potential. Griffin would never admit this, but Vetch was learning noticeably faster than all the rest and seemed to have had a bow in his hand his whole life.

After the third day of training, Griffin was eavesdropping on Sable and Mogol. The two of them sat around a circular table in the room next to Sable's in the castle. They seemed to be speaking of something of great importance and had a large piece of parchment set before them. The boy sat to the side of the door so the two beings could not see him. Griffin could only hear segments of the conversation. Mogol announced, "Our soldiers will silently fly in and surround the lake on all sides. And while they attack, they must stay airborne. The key is to stay in the air but still be able to pursue them. This is how we will keep our numbers up and claim victory."

"Yes, yes, this is great preparation. I will show Vetch the battle plans, and we will go to war tomorrow," Sable replied.

"But so soon? But are you sure?"

"With Adria missing, they must be seeking to attack soon."

"You know, no good comes to secretly listening to other people's conversations."

Alarmed, Griffin jumped to the side. "A–Adria." Griffin gripped her hand and took her away from the room where Sable and Mogol were plotting the battle.

"What? What is it?"

Griffin led her into his room and announced, "We are going to battle … tomorrow."

Adria cocked her head to one side and said, "What? Already? But are they ready, Griffin?"

Griffin sat down on his bed. He thought to himself for a few seconds. "Well…I guess they haven't shown me they aren't ready. They have learned amazingly fast. I can't believe how well they can use a bow. It just seems soon."

"But you see, Griffin," Adria began, "Sable doesn't have much of a choice." She sat down in the wooden chair next to the table. "You see, the Shriekian haven't attacked the Critins for nearly a month. Sable knows they must be scheming to attack soon. That is why we must attack first, before they do."

Griffin ran his fingers past his wounded cheek and through his shaggy hair. "Adria, but what if they *aren't* ready? What if the whole bow idea doesn't work? Or–or what if it's a total disaster, and it's all my fault? And–and…"

Adria stood up and clasped her hand over his mouth. "You have been nothing but a faithful teacher to them. Don't doubt yourself; you have done all you can. You have brought hope to this race."

She took her hand off his mouth. Griffin smiled then replied, "Well, I guess we will find out tomorrow."

IT IS TIME

"Soldiers, this day is ours! The Shriekian will at last pay for what they have brought to our kind!" Sable spoke to the army moments before they were to fly into battle. His words echoed powerfully throughout the Oval. "Each one of you has suffered grave tragedies from these wretched creatures. Now is our time to rise up and bring them down for what they have bestowed upon us!" The Critin army breathed heavily, allowing their breath to be seen in the early morning air. They all were restless. "You shall fight for the honor of the Critin race. Vetch has the battle plans that you will follow. My warriors, it is time!"

Griffin and Adria stood restlessly next to Sable as he spoke to them. The army gathered in a large circle to look over the battle procedures. With his shortbow in hand and quiver on his back, Griffin approached the conversing warriors. "Where do you think you are going?" Adria asked Griffin.

The boy kept treading nearer to the army and answered, "I'm going to see how I can help."

"Are you crazy?"

Griffin did not answer as he advanced to the gathered soldiers. Vetch turned to him. "What do you want, human?"

"I want to go with you."

Vetch leaned closer to Griffin's face. "There is no place for a human in my army. Best stay back where it's safe."

"If the boy wishes to help, let him! He can use these weapons better than any of us!" a soldier in the crowd yelled.

Vetch turned to the Critin who had made the suggestion and snapped, "There is *no* place for a human in my army. If you think otherwise, you can join him in the castle." Vetch circled back to Griffin. "Now, please leave my presence!" Griffin glared into Vetch's eyes with disgust then stormed out of the Oval; the enraged boy slammed the door shut as he left the castle top.

The impatient soldiers looked at the battle plans for a few minutes longer and then took flight, making two single–file lines as they flew. Vetch soared in the middle, at the front of the two rows of soldiers. The sack of arrows hung down by their feathered bellies, and their arms were occupied with carrying their bow. The army's wings waved up and down in long strides, covering ground in a short amount of time. Never once did they fall out of line. They were soundless, focused, and most of all prepared for what was to come.

Many miles later they reached the Shriekian Lake. The mighty Shriekian castle was not protruding from the green water, and there was no sign of life coming from the lake. The Critins plummeted toward the swampy depths. Using their wings, they hovered at the start of the water, and Vetch motioned with his arms to his troops to circle the lake. They did as they were told, making sure not a sound escaped them. The army stayed airborne as they waited for Vetch's next signal. Vetch hovered at the front of the lake where the castle doors would point to when it came to surface. The army leader carefully took an arrow in hand and placed it on the strings of the bow. Now surrounding the lake on all sides, the army did the same as Vetch. He then pulled back on the strings and, still in complete silence, pointed the unforgiving arrow toward the middle of the body of water. They all followed his lead. All eyes were locked on the center of the lake. They hovered patiently, waiting for Vetch's word.

Vetch bellowed, "Fire!" Fifty arrows released into the murky depths of the lake. The water became uneasy as the arrows penetrated deep into the water. The army immediately reset their bows and prepared themselves to set free another volley. Not the slightest sign of life came from the lake. The ripples of small waves that the arrows caused slowly died down. Vetch once again shouted so all could hear, "Fire!" The ammo sliced through the liquid with much force, once again causing the water to turn wavy. "Hold your fire!" The Critins, trying to anticipate what was to come, were overwhelmed with a rumbling sensation building deep inside the Shriekian Lake. The rumbling grew more severe by the second, and soon the earth began to suffer from a mighty quake. A numerous amount of bubbles rose to the murky surface of the green–tinted water, and waves splashed up at the flying Critin army.

The soldiers' catlike eyes stayed focused on the middle of the lake when a black, pointed tip began to emerge from it. A structure much greater in size followed the pointed tip as the Shriekian castle slowly rose to the surface.

"Hold fire!" Vetch shouted. The warriors continued to position their arrows toward the rising black castle. The Shriekian domain took well over half the lake when it finally came into view. Diluted water washed out of its black, forbidding walls, and the lake served as a moat protecting the fortress.

Greenish blue fins started to extend beyond the water's surface and sink back down. All around the lake, fins jolted up then sank down, sprang out of the water then went down. *"Do not shoot until they are fully surfaced!"* Vetch warned. Every indication of the Shriekian army had disappeared when suddenly a creature slowly emerged its rubbery head from the water. The Shriekian contained enormous alien eyes and a slick, long head used for treading through water with ease. The being snapped his unforgiving fangs together as he waded in the water before Vetch. In the water, the lone Shriekian felt he was out of harm's way and hissed, "What do you think your kind is doing? Leave our soil or suffer greatly."

Pointing his arrow at the water beast, Vetch replied, "It is your time to suffer." He released his talons from the extended bow string, and the arrow hurled straight into the eye of the creature, killing it instantly. As soon as the Shriekian corpse began to submerge to the rock bottom, the Shriekian army attacked.

Vetch bellowed, *"Fire at will!"* Using their slippery tail fins to spring out of the water, the creatures attempted to bring down the airborne beings. It looked like fish making an effort to leap out of the water for an insect meal. Their tail fins transformed into two mutantlike legs with clawed feet as soon as their scale–covered bodies left the lake. The Shriekian clasped their jagged teeth together as they strived to snatch the feathered beings down to watery graves.

Arrow upon powerful arrow rained down on the lake as more and more Shriekians surfaced to fight. The castle's drawbridge gave way, and flock of water beings dove to the lake, causing their legs to be turned back into large tail fins.

Lifeless Shriekian bodies bobbed up and down, making it more difficult for the creatures to move about the murky water. Vetch drove the missiles into their flesh, executing an uncountable number of the Shriekian.

Glancing at a fellow soldier, Vetch demanded, *"Do not get too close to the water!"* Before the endangered Critin could react, it was taken over by two of the enraged water creatures. Its right talon was completely consumed in the mouth of a Shriekian, and it was taken deep beneath the lake's surface, surely never to return. Vetch commanded once again, *"Warriors, do not stray near the surface of the lake!"*

The Critin army was relentless against the ones who had made them suffer so immensely. They showed no mercy. Their minds contained one intention only—to destroy.

The Shriekian continued to make feeble attempts to take them over until a desperate water creature motioned his webbed hand toward Vetch and screamed, *"Bring that one down!"*

A pack of twenty Shriekian monsters swiftly swam beneath the water toward Vetch, causing water to spray upward in their pursuit. One Shriekian used the large wake they had made to launch itself toward the hovering Vetch. Predicting the Shriekians' intensions, Vetch swiped his wings up in hopes to be out of their range. He was not high enough. The angry Shriekian enclosed his mighty jaws entirely around Vetch's feathered leg. He roared with pain as he uncontrollably began to plummet to the many snapping jaws of the Shriekian below.

Refusing to give in, Vetch hurriedly motioned his wings up and down through the air. But there was no use as he was slowly pulled closer to the polluted water. Suddenly an arrow whizzed past Vetch's resisting body. The arrow struck through the neck of the Shriekian that had Vetch restrained. With an ear–piercing shriek, the creature released Vetch's leg, which was now covered in blood. In a state of panic, Vetch rap-idly flapped his wings upward and out of the creature's reach. He rotated his body around to see who had saved his life. Flying about the uneasy lake was Snolan, and she carried on her back none other than Griffin. She soared about the premises as Griffin brought down Shriekian after Shriekian. Griffin released his arrows, impelling them into the heads, necks, and bod-ies of the wretched animals. The boy wrapped his legs tightly around the torso of the dragon as he continued to end the enemies' lives.

"Snolan, a bit lower!" Griffin shouted.

They circled the Shriekian castle, killing all they could in their path. The combination of Griffin, Snolan, and the whole Critin army was beginning to be too much for the once mighty army, and it was starting to show. The muddy lake was now covered with floating carcasses of the overpowered Shriekian army.

The rumbling sound began once more, and the dark castle started to sink back down to the depths. Following the castle down to the rock bottom was the remainder of the Shriekian army. They had surrendered. The mighty Shriekian race swam deep into the water in hopes of finding refuge. Looking about the mass of lifeless bodies consuming the lake, Griffin exclaimed, "Snolan! Snolan, they gave up! They left!"

"They sure did, Griffin!" the dragon proudly replied as she hurled her wings toward the bank of the lake. The Critin army realized what had just occurred, and they gathered in the air, shouting in mass celebration.

Griffin watched them as he recognized what he had done for this species. He had brought them hope; he had brought them dreams. This boy had brought them life.

THE NEW BEGINNING

Griffin flew on the back of Snolan, trailing the rest of the army. There was an endless chatter throughout the enthralled warriors. Vetch was still at the front of the pack, his wounded leg dangling below him.

The army soared through the Critin village as the villagers below cheered and cried their gratitude toward their warriors. They landed on the castle top, and the army spoke no words as Sable approached Vetch. "Sir," Vetch spoke to him, "the beasts retreated to the bottom of the Shriekian domain. We slaughtered many. The battle is won." Sable beamed at the soldiers with such love and gratefulness. The day he thought he would never see had finally arrived.

"You have done it, my soldiers!" Sable shouted to all. "The Shriekian have just been given a small piece of what is yet to come. We will *not* let down! They will now fear us! Fear is what their future holds! Prosperity is what ours holds!" They all shouted in approval and raised their bows to the sky. Sable glanced down to Vetch's injured leg. There were five large bite marks around his leg and talon. "You must give that attention immediately," Sable told him.

Vetch looked to the ground. "It could have been much worse if–if the kid hadn't of come."

"What? Griffin followed you?"

"Yes. And if he hadn't, I would not be standing before you, Sable. Griffin! Step up here."

Griffin walked from behind the gathered army of Critins. He stopped in front of Vetch and Sable.

Griffin hurriedly explained, "Look, I just felt like I had to go. I'm sorr—"

"This boy disobeyed yours and my orders, Sable," Vetch sternly announced. Vetch turned to Griffin. "And for that you have saved my life."

The castle doors began to open, and Adria stepped through them. Her eyes locked on Griffin, and she ran to him. Adria wrapped her arms around Griffin, nearly causing him to drop his shortbow. She didn't release him for a great while, and he hugged her back. Finally letting go, Adria said with relief, "I didn't know if you were going to come back."

Griffin smiled back at her. "Well, I'm here, aren't I?" Griffin joked. "You don't need to watch over me."

Adria smiled softly and replied, "Well, some-one has to."

There was a grand feast and a mass festival to celebrate the dawning of a new era. Every-one in the Critin village gathered to rejoice this newfound life. Apprehension was no longer a factor as the Critin race began to feel free and live without fear.

Griffin himself felt liberated and, most of all, loved and appreciated. The boy wished he could somehow share with John what these past few days have brought him, but he knew it wasn't possible. One could see a change in the villagers, for they did not have the hatred that they once had for humans.

When the celebration ended, Griffin and Adria gazed out into the open land at the Oval. "This is all unreal," Adria said as she looked to Griffin.

"What is?"

She moved her hair out of her face, and, squinting her eyes, she exclaimed, "What do you mean what is? This…bringing down the Shriekian, helping the Critins, being here with you, it just seems…"

"Impossible?"

"Yes, yes, impossible."

"Adria," Griffin said, "this isn't a coincidence. This happened to us for a reason. We are here together because it was inevitable. Can you feel it?"

"Yes." She smiled.

Turning away from her, Griffin softly snickered. "Besides, who else was going to save you?"

Adria rolled her eyes and laughed a bit. "Well, I'm going to get ready for bed. See you in the morning." She started toward the door.

"Good night. And Adria…?" She turned back to him. "I'm glad I have someone to watch over me."

She beamed at Griffin for a moment then said, "I'll see you in the morning." She exited the Oval.

Moments after she left him, Sable came through the doors. Griffin knew it was Sable before turning to face him, for the red glare of the diamond shone brightly in the crisp night. "I have never before seen the happiness in my people that they have shown today."

"They deserve to not live in fear," Griffin stated.

"Yes, Griffin, and you have made this probable for my kind."

"You keep saying I have brought hope to your race, Sable, when I'm the one who never wants to leave here. I never want to leave Aranwea," Griffin told him. His long hair rustled in the soft breeze. Griffin looked to Sable, expecting to see happiness, but this was not what he found. Sable's eyes drooped, and he appeared doubtful. Griffin questioned, "Sable, we won the battle. The Shriekian retreated. What's wrong?"

Sable spoke no words. The diamond carrier continued to look at into the vast land of Aranwea. Sable seemed to be completely engulfed in his deepest thoughts. Many moments later, he confessed, "Yes, Griffin, the battle is won. But I fear something much bigger is rapidly approaching, for I am afraid we have awakened a sleeping beast."

Griffin studied Sable's reaction a bit. *They are finally becoming a free race,* the boy thought to himself. "Sable, we may have awakened them, but I see something larger awakening in the Critin race ... hope."

e|LIVE

---

listen|imagine|view|experience

AUDIO BOOK DOWNLOAD INCLUDED WITH THIS BOOK!

In your hands you hold a complete digital entertainment package. In addition to the paper version, you receive a free download of the audio version of this book. Simply use the code listed below when visiting our website. Once downloaded to your computer, you can listen to the book through your computer's speakers, burn it to an audio CD or save the file to your portable music device (such as Apple's popular iPod) and listen on the go!

How to get your free audio book digital download:

1. Visit www.tatepublishing.com and click on the e|LIVE logo on the home page.
2. Enter the following coupon code:
   d89f-3fcd-d215-04a5-3cad-e727-c9ed-71c5
3. Download the audio book from your e|LIVE digital locker and begin enjoying your new digital entertainment package today!